SARAH'S LEGACY

DAISY BEILER TOWNSEND

Dedication

To the memory of my mother, Ruth M. Beiler, who left me and all her children and grandchildren a legacy of prayer.

To Jane

God bless you as you leave a godly legacy.

Daisy Townsend
3/8/18

Acknowledgements

I want to thank my husband, Donn, for his help, patience, prayers and support during the writing and publishing of this book. I am so blessed by all you do and are.

Thanks to Doug Williams for his timely help on the cover of Sarah's Legacy. We were stuck!

Also, a huge thank you to the ACFW Scribes who critiqued Sarah's Legacy, especially Laurie Germaine (from whom I learned so much), Esther Bandy (who has since become my dear friend), Gwen Hartzler (who said, "You absolutely CAN do it yourself!), and Loraine Hunsaker (who also gave me valuable information on self-publishing).

A big thank you as well to my faithful prayer partners during the process of this book, my daughter, Angelyn Trumbull, Bonnie Prugh, Cherri McAnallen, DeVonne White, MaryElla Young, and Stacey Pardoe. What a blessing you've been!

I also must thank Isabel Dye, who has since passed away, for telling me the story behind the history of our former home in Sandy Lake, Pennsylvania. Without her, this story would not have been written.

Disclaimer

Sarah's Legacy was inspired by the Thomas and Sarah Davis family and the Robert and Margaret Dye family. They lived at 259 Broad Street (now 81 Broad Street) in Sandy Lake, Pennsylvania, in the late 1800's and early 1900's—our home from 1988 to 2008. You will also encounter other professionals and residents who lived in Sandy Lake during that era.

In spite of the fact that the Davis', the Dye's, and several other characters were real people, and that some of the events in this book actually happened, the characters I've created and the story I've written are a work of fiction.

CHAPTER 1

February 1910
Sandy Lake, Pennsylvania

Polly burst through the front door of the large, two-story house. A sudden chill of apprehension stopped her exuberant rush. She shivered. Sunlight flooded the faded red and gray wallpapered room. It glistened off the leaded window beside the door, at odds with the darkness and oppression.

Footsteps pounded across the porch as the rest of the family pushed past her with loud, excited exclamations. The younger children raced through the empty rooms and up the stairs with Polly close behind.

"Florence."

The urgency of Mother's voice squelched Polly's enthusiasm just as effectively as the strange foreboding had a moment before. She teetered on the bottom step. Why wouldn't her parents call her Polly as everyone else did?

She turned. Her mother, white-faced and weary, with Twila in one arm and Elsie clutching her other hand, stood in the doorway. Polly sprinted toward her, irritation forgotten. "Let me take the baby. Maggie, you keep an eye on Elsie."

Polly nudged Elsie in Maggie's direction as Maggie trailed in behind their mother, book in hand.

"Look, here's an old chair. Why don't you sit and rest while we take care of the children?"

Her mother surrendered Twila and Elsie and sank into the dilapidated green chair. "Thank you, Florence. I don't know what I'd do without you."

"You'll feel better after we're settled." Polly squeezed her mother's shoulder. Twila would soon be a year old. Shouldn't Mother have regained her strength by now?

She settled Twila's plump body on her hip as Papa and Ben came through the door.

"Do you think the house is solid and well built, Papa?" Ben's voice squeaked into a falsetto.

Polly looked past them, hoping to spot Garrett. He'd promised to help with moving today. Not that her mother would be happy to see him. Polly glanced at her. Had she forgotten Garrett's promise?

"Yes, Ben, I think..."

Polly twirled herself and Twila through the archway, away from Ben and Papa's boring conversation and Mother's too-penetrating eyes. She swooped and swirled in the middle of the empty dining room, a lock of red hair escaping from her wool hat. Their oak dining room table and chairs would look splendid next to the sunny window. She yanked off her hat and tossed it into the air before pirouetting into the kitchen with Twila's giggles surrounding her. Maybe one day she and Garrett...

She closed her eyes against the familiar inner tug. If only Mother... "*No.*" Twila jerked at the explosive sound and Polly opened her eyes. Twila popped her thumb in her mouth, alarmed question marks in her blue gaze. She patted Twila's cheek and added silently, "I *will* enjoy this day."

Hugging her little sister close, Polly looked around the kitchen. Nothing unusual here, but it was the feeling of space she loved most about this house. So much bigger than their house in the country which seemed to shrink each time a new brother or sister arrived.

Perhaps in this house that feeling would go away. Perhaps here she...

The chilling sensation she'd had when she entered the house gripped her again. She had no words to describe it. Maybe Mother was right—maybe she had an overactive imagination.

Polly jumped when Twila clapped her hands and peered at her. "Sorry, baby dear. Let's go see how Mama's doing."

As she retraced her steps, unfamiliar voices came from the living room. The aroma of a freshly baked pie tantalized her nostrils. A slim, blue-eyed man with a streak of blue paint on his cheek and a dark-complexioned woman in a red, wool coat and multi-colored scarf stood by the door.

"Florence, I'd like you to meet our next-door neighbors—Blanche and Harry. They can't stay because they're going somewhere with their sons, Vance and—What was your other son's name?"

"William." Blanche smiled at Polly.

"This is our oldest daughter, Florence..."

"Just call me Polly, everyone does—everyone except Mother and Father. That pie smells delicious."

"I hope you'll like it. Apple's our favorite."

"Mine, too." Polly sniffed again.

"We'd better go." Harry reached for the doorknob. "The boys are waiting."

Blanche turned toward him, then looked again. "Bet you can't guess what Harry does for a living, huh?" She chuckled. "Nice to meet you folks." The door closed behind them.

Mother raised a puzzled eyebrow at Polly.

Polly giggled. "Didn't you see the paint on Harry's cheek?"

"Oh, I understand. He must be a painter."

Squatting beside Mother's chair, Polly balanced Twila precariously on her knee. "Are you feeling better?"

"I feel much stronger, dear. Twila will be all right here with me now that Papa has built a fire in the wood stove. Would you put this pie on the radiator, please? There's no fire in the coal furnace yet."

Taking off her coat, Polly spread it on the floor and settled Twila with a gentle plop, as the wood stove's warmth permeated the room. As she transferred the pie, Mother glanced at her. "Why don't you go upstairs and check on the other children."

Her pulse quickened as Polly peeked into the small sitting room to her right and then took the steps two at a time to the unexplored realm above. Even the familiar sound of Robert and George arguing, Beth chiming in now and then, couldn't dim her enthusiasm.

"Polly."

She sighed and went straight to the third room on the right where Robert and George stood toe to toe, voices raised. "Why are you arguing?"

"Robert says he's going to sleep in this bedroom." George's voice took on a high-pitched whine. "But I like this room best and *I* want to sleep here."

"I'm older so I should get first choice." Robert pulled himself up to his full height—an inch taller than George.

George scowled. "Only two years."

"There aren't enough bedrooms for each of us to have a room. If Mother says it's all right, you can both sleep in this room."

"What about me, Polly?" Beth jumped up and down.

"We're sick of sharing." George looked at his brother who nodded agreement.

"You boys need to be thankful you have a roof over your heads." Polly cringed. That's what her mother had said to her when she'd complained about the house in the country.

She turned back to Beth and patted her sister's long, brown braids. "As for you, we'll have to ask Mama later where she wants you to sleep."

Leaving the boys to their bickering, Polly scurried from the room with Beth on her heels. Maggie and Elsie passed them, headed for the steps. "Hold her hand on the way down, Maggie."

Maggie shrugged but took Elsie's hand.

Across the hall from the green room, Polly and Beth found a smaller, drab-looking room that gave the impression of being totally brown.

"This room is ugly." Beth turned up her nose. "It looks like vomit."

"You're right. I hope I don't get stuck with this room." Again, she heard the echo of her mother's words as they moved into the next bedroom. *You ought to be thankful you have a roof over your head.*

"I guess I'm as bad as the boys." Polly sighed. *Just once, I wish I could think of myself without feeling guilty.*

As she moved into the next room, a floorboard moved and creaked beneath her feet. "My goodness." Polly's voice echoed in the empty room. "For a 'solid, well-built house,' that didn't feel very safe."

"Maybe it's a ghost." Beth giggled.

"Mother says there's no such thing as ghosts."

Startled out of her brief bout of rebellion, Polly looked at what she already thought of as "the back bedroom," secluded and sheltered.

"Look, Polly." Beth pointed at the wallpaper. "Your favorite colors—yellow and green."

"The splashes of color remind me of ferns and sunshine." Polly stroked the smooth walls. "I think this wallpaper is new."

"Maybe this can be your room."

"Maybe. Or at least mine and Maggie's. Unless..."

"Unless what?"

"Unless Papa and Mama want this room. The little brown room connected to it would make a wonderful nursery." Polly sighed again, a long, drawn-out sound that came from deep in her soul. At the same time, she tingled all over with an unexplainable foreboding. Much as it repelled her, she forced herself to focus on it. *I can't decide whether something bad has happened here or something bad is going to happen.*

Horse's hoofs clattered outside the window. Polly's despondency evaporated as she ran to see who had arrived, her feet somehow finding once more the board with the unsettling squeak.

CHAPTER 2

Polly raced down the stairs and out the front door, ignoring Mother's protest. "Florence, your coat—it's cold out there."

"Garrett, oh Garrett, you came."

"Course I came." Garrett Young's blue eyes sparkled as he jumped down from Polly's Uncle Jim's wagon. "I promised I'd help move the furniture today."

"When you didn't show up at the other house, I thought maybe you'd forgotten." Polly shivered and pushed her hands inside the heavy, woolen material of her long-sleeved green dress.

"I got a late start this morning—hard to get out of bed on such a cold day. I caught up with your uncle just as he was leaving."

"You'd better get in the house, Florence, before you catch your death." Uncle Jim started back toward the wagon loaded with furniture. "Tell your Pa and the boys we're here to help unload your stuff."

Polly trudged up the steps, glancing over her shoulder at Garrett. As she reached the door, Father and the boys streamed out, calling greetings to Garrett and Uncle Jim.

"I'll get my coat and come back to help." Polly stepped over the threshold.

"You'd better stay indoors to help Mother with the little ones." Father's brows drew together. "She seems all tired out today."

"But Garrett's here. Why can't Maggie help Mother?"

"Mother needs both of you today."

"But..."

"Florence, let's not argue."

Mother still sat on the unsightly green chair with Twila clinging to her skirts as Polly shuffled past. She warmed her hands at the now-glowing woodstove. The fragrance of the apple pie still hung in the air. "Garrett came to help, Mother. Wasn't that good of him?"

Pursing her lips, Mother glanced out the window. "I thought he promised to come in time to help *load* the furniture."

"Well, yes but..." Polly's voice trailed away. "I guess he just...got a late start."

After a long silence, Polly took a few steps toward her mother. "Why do you dislike Garrett so much?"

"I don't *dislike* him exactly." Mother wrinkled her forehead and repositioned herself on the rickety chair. "It's just that I'm not sure I trust him."

Before Polly could respond, Mother spoke again. "Now I have a question for you. Why do you *like* Garrett so much?"

It was Polly's turn to wrinkle her forehead. She'd never stopped to think about why she liked Garrett. "I guess—" She hesitated. "I guess it's because he's fun. He makes me laugh, and he likes to have a good time."

"I know your life seems dull sometimes. I depend on you a lot to help keep the family going. Fun isn't a top priority, and I'm not sure it's much of a foundation for a serious relationship."

"No one said it's a serious relationship." Polly squirmed and backed up a few steps under Mother's direct gaze.

"You've been spending a lot of time together. Is it fair to lead Garrett on if you're not serious?"

Twila started to fuss, a sleepy cry. Polly moved to pick her up. Maggie's voice from upstairs with Elsie and Beth competed with men's laughter and boys' shrill voices as they unloaded the wagon. Mother's statement hung in the air.

"I don't think I'm leading Garrett on. I don't know whether I'm serious about him or whether he's serious about me. We go ice skating and take sleigh rides or whatever we can find to do that's fun. I don't think there's anything wrong with that."

Polly's cheeks warmed. What she'd told Mother was true, but not the whole truth. She wasn't ready to talk about the kisses she and Garrett exchanged in his father's buggy. Or the strange feelings the kisses generated in the pit of her stomach. Mother would probably think those kisses qualified as a serious relationship.

Happy for a reason to end the conversation, Polly opened the door allowing Father and Uncle James to bring in the dining room table. Still Mother's question nagged her. Was she leading Garrett on?

♠

That night Polly fell into bed, muscles aching and mind racing as she lay awake in the wide, four-poster bed she shared with Maggie and Beth. The question she'd been avoiding all day now confronted her. In spite of the kisses they shared, why didn't she think her relationship with Garrett was serious?

Maybe because she and Garrett were seldom serious about anything. Had they ever had a serious conversation? Even after kissing her, Garrett usually made some teasing remark about her warm lips helping to take the chill out of the night. He never said anything tender, loving or even particularly meaningful. Never said anything about his feelings for her.

Her conclusions would not be comforting to Mother. She wouldn't approve of Polly exchanging kisses with someone who had never given her reason to believe he was serious. Kissing wasn't something her mother would look on as a legitimate way of "having fun."

Turning to her right side, Polly opened her eyes, making out the bureau and blanket chest in the dark room. Her parents had chosen the back bedroom so Mother could be near Elsie and Twila in the adjoining smaller room. Robert and George had agreed to share the green room since that was the only way they could both have what they wanted. Polly, Maggie, and Beth took the lavender room. Ben, the only one to obtain that coveted prize, a room of his own—small as it was—had the blue room at the top of the stairs.

He hadn't gotten that room without a heated debate with Polly. She had finally yielded because George and Robert's bickering drove Ben crazy. She didn't really mind sharing a room, though she'd been disappointed about not having the yellow and green one. Not that she'd allowed her disappointment to show. Mother had enough problems.

Maybe some day when I'm married, I'll have the nicest room to share with my *husband.* What would it be like to be married to Garrett? She squirmed. Strange she'd never thought about being married to Garrett. It made her uncomfortable. Not that she didn't like the idea of being married, but she couldn't picture Garrett in the role of husband and father. Maybe because of the comparison with her own father.

Although Garrett worked at the Sandy Lake Gristmill for his cousin, Irvin, he found many reasons to skip work. If he wasn't part of the family, Polly suspected his cousin would've fired him. Polly's father on the other hand, always worked hard to provide for their family. He enjoyed a good laugh, but didn't let anything interfere with his responsibilities.

Perhaps it wasn't fair to compare Garrett with her father. If Garrett were married and had a family to support, maybe he'd be more responsible. Maybe earning money wasn't important to him because he lived with his parents.

Turning on her other side, Polly took comfort from Beth's warm body next to hers, sniffing her little girl fragrance. She drifted off to sleep, dreaming of Garrett's warm kisses. They blotted out everything else, including the words of warning her mother had spoken.

CHAPTER 3

"Don't be late." Mother watched Polly with that tinge of worry in her eyes that appeared when Polly was going out with Garrett.

Polly planted a loving kiss on her mother's cheek as she swooped up her sweater and streaked for the door. She hoped to avoid an argument about what was proper if Garrett didn't come up to the house.

The warm May breeze caressed her face as she ran down the porch steps and reveled in the joy of being outdoors without the heavy trappings of winter. The air smelled fresh and clean from the afternoon rain.

"Hi Beautiful." Garrett's eyes shone with approval as Polly stepped into his father's buggy.

She murmured a greeting, feeling a little shy under the intensity of his searching gaze. It was almost as though he saw her for the first time. It *was* the first time this spring he'd seen her without her winter hat and coat.

Garrett clucked to the shiny black purebred horses which started at a brisk trot. "I'm surprised your mother let you come out with me again tonight."

Polly tensed. "You know my mother's health hasn't been good. The move was hard on her. Since I'm the oldest, I'm often needed at home."

"What about Maggie? She's sixteen, isn't she old enough to help?"

"Maggie is so easily distracted by her books that when Mother doesn't feel well, it's easier for her if I'm there to keep

Maggie moving."

Garrett frowned.

"Mother is much stronger now. That's why I'm able to spend more time with you."

Before Garrett could open his mouth with any more complaints, Polly lifted her face to catch the magic of the warm breeze on her cheeks. "Isn't spring wonderful? I can't believe winter is over. I hope we never have snow again."

As she turned toward Garrett, his gaze held the same passion she'd sensed before. Was he going to tell her he loved her? But Garrett just chuckled. "A few months ago, you were raving about how beautiful the snowflakes were."

"Oh I know." Her shoulders drooped. "Right now I'm just tired of winter—so tired of keeping track of all the boots and scarves and mittens. Beth and George are always losing things."

"Can't your mother help them now that she's feeling better?"

"You're an only child. You don't understand what it's like to live in a big family. Everyone has to help. It would be ridiculous to expect Mother to do everything."

This was as close as Polly and Garrett had ever come to quarreling. She hated it but she couldn't allow Garrett to insinuate Mother was lazy. "Why are you so critical of my mother?"

"She's the one who's critical. She told me my manners needed improvement."

They glared at each other. Then Garrett threw back his head and laughed, becoming the happy-go-lucky self Polly loved. "You're even prettier when you're mad." He put his arm around her and pulled her close.

Polly tried to pull away. "It's still daylight."

Glancing around at the tree-lined road, Garrett pulled Polly even closer. "Who's going to see us out here in the country?" He leaned over and kissed her mouth.

"I mean it. Stop."

"What's the matter? You liked my kisses well enough before."

Polly pulled free and retreated as far as the narrow buggy seat allowed. "Not in broad daylight. It... It doesn't seem right."

"You sound just like your mother." Garrett twisted the

reins around one hand and crossed his arms. "Why is it any worse to kiss in daylight than after dark?"

Wrinkling her forehead, Polly pulled on her sweater. "I don't know. Maybe it's wrong either way."

Stopping the horses, Garrett gave Polly his full attention. He stared at her and shook his head. "What's wrong with kissing?"

The silence grew long except for the slow, steady whip-poor-will, whip-poor-will in the dense woods. "I guess there's nothing wrong with kissing if two people are serious about each other."

"I go out with you every chance I get. Doesn't that count as serious?"

"I don't know." Polly bit her lip. "We never talk about anything serious except when you're complaining about my mother, and—" Her voice faded away.

"And what?"

She forced herself to look into Garrett's piercing blue eyes. "And you've never said you love me or that you want to marry me." There, it was out at last. The issue they needed to talk about so she'd know whether this was a serious relationship.

Garrett's gaze slid away from hers. "Of course we're going to get married—someday. I'm just not ready to settle down."

"My mother was married by the time *she* was 18." Polly shivered a little. The sun's rays were fading and she felt chilled even with her sweater. Garrett had not said he loved her. He had said they were going to get married "someday." He hadn't answered her question.

"Come here, Pretty Lady. You're way too far away." Garrett pulled her against him. "If we wait a few minutes, it'll be dark, then maybe I can kiss you without you making a fuss." He patted her shoulder.

It was no use. Garrett didn't get it. But even with her insides churning, she responded to his touch. She loved to be hugged and kissed, and it felt good to relax against his strong shoulder. Surely there could be nothing wrong with that.

"Have I told you how beautiful you look tonight?" Garrett tilted her chin so he could look deep into her eyes. "Did you know the green in your dress matches the green of your eyes?"

It was the sweetest thing he had ever said to her. Tears

gathered at his tender tone. She snuggled closer to him as he continued to gaze into her eyes. This time when he lowered his lips to hers, she didn't resist.

♠

A light still glowed through the living room window. Polly crept up the front porch steps, not sure whether she was relieved to see it or not. No light might mean Mother and Father were angry that she'd stayed out so late, but a light could mean she'd have to talk to her mother about where she'd been.

She breathed a sigh of relief as she saw the empty gray armchair where Mother usually sat—then almost knocked over a stool when a voice from the other side of the room startled her. Father had been watching from the chair in the shadowy corner.

"Father. I didn't see you."

He rubbed his hand over his chin with the raspy sound of late night whiskers. "It's late, Florence."

Polly stopped smiling as she looked at his weary face. How could she have been so thoughtless? "I'm so sorry. Truly I am. Garrett and I... We were having such fun. I lost all track of time."

The lines in Father's face softened. "You're a good girl, Florence. You work hard, and you need to have fun. But you know your mother. She worries about you. The only way I could get her to go to bed was if I promised to stay up until you came home. I don't want her to get all worn out again."

Polly kissed her father's scratchy cheek. "I'm sorry I was so late. I promise I'll try to do better."

Although her father didn't particularly approve of Garrett either, he was too preoccupied with problems at the mine to get involved. She yawned as they started up the stairs. Maybe by morning she would be ready to answer the questions she knew her mother would ask.

CHAPTER 4

Garrett rolled over, opened one sleepy eye, and then snapped it shut to block out the sunshine streaming in his window. It must be late. Oh well. Irvin knew he always ran late. If Garrett was supposed to open the store, Irvin always scheduled someone else to come in early, too. One of those unspoken issues everyone understood.

He sniffed. Was his mother frying bacon? He put both feet on the floor and yawned and stretched. So tempting to crawl back into bed for a few more minutes. Rubbing his eyes, he blinked and ran his hands through his bronze-blond hair. A late night but certainly worth it.

After dragging a pair of heavy work socks out of his bureau drawer, he slumped on the edge of his bed. Polly was all right—a few old-fashioned ideas she'd picked up from her mother but things were coming along fine. Last night was the best yet in spite of getting off to a rough start. Although he liked to keep things light, he'd have to remember that Polly liked some sweet-talking, too.

Sweet-talking was tricky. You had to find just the right combination for every girl. Enough to get them in the right mood without making any promises.

He leaned over to pick up his second sock. He'd better move a little faster or he might get a lecture when he got to the mill. He made short work of the rest of his morning ritual, except for getting his hair just right, and ran whistling down the long flight of stairs into the warm, sunny kitchen.

Standing with her back to him, Ma took long, thick slabs of bacon from the heavy iron skillet. Her face was rosy from the heat of the stove as he sneaked up behind her to plant a kiss on her cheek. "Morning, Ma. You look grand this morning."

"Garrett." His mother tried to frown, even as she beamed at his compliment and heaped food on a heavy blue and gray plate, "Weren't you supposed to open the store this morning?"

"Ah, Ma, don't worry. You know Irv always covers me on my days to open." He took the plate heaped with bacon, fried potatoes and two fried eggs.

"I didn't hear you come in last night. What time did you get home?"

"I don't know. I forgot to wind my watch." Garrett sat down at the small claw-footed table by the window.

"Where were you?"

"Oh Ma, why all the questions? I was just out with some of the fellows."

"I thought you said you were going out with Polly."

Garrett frowned as his mother brought him a tall, cold glass of milk. "Why did you ask if you knew I was with her? Don't you trust me?"

"But Garrett..." His mother blinked as she always did when he turned the tables on her.

"I only said..." He chewed and swallowed part of the load of food he'd just shoveled into his mouth. "I only said I was with the guys to see whether you were trying to trick me."

His mother wiped her hands on a dish towel and sat down beside him. "I'm sorry. I shouldn't have asked where you were. I get worried when I wake up in the night and haven't heard you come in. If you'd let me wait up for you, I wouldn't worry so much."

He washed down his last mouthful of food with another big gulp of milk. "You know how *I'd* worry about *you* if you were waiting up for me. I wouldn't be able to have any fun if I thought you weren't getting enough sleep."

Garrett patted his mother's chapped hands and her eyes glowed.

"You're always so considerate of me. I'll try not to worry and fuss so much."

He got up and kissed his mother's cheek. "I've got to hurry now so Irv doesn't take a sniveling fit."

The sun smiled on him as he walked to the gristmill. *What a shame to waste such a nice day working.* For a minute, he was tempted to go back and get his fishing pole and head for the creek. He hesitated. Maybe that would be pushing it a little. Old Irvin had gotten pretty riled a couple times lately. Not that Irv would actually fire him.

Better not take a chance. If he had to look for a job somewhere else, he might have to work a lot harder than he did at the mill.

Garrett went in the front entrance instead of the back where the workers usually came in. Less chance of his cousin seeing him from the office this way. Then if Irv yelled at him for being late, Garrett could tell him he'd come in the front door and been there a long time already.

At first the store seemed deserted. Then young, lilting female voices drifted from the back of the store, so he strode in that direction. Women didn't often come here. One of the drawbacks of this job.

As he rounded the corner, two attractive, shapely young women were talking to an older man. Garrett smoothed his thick hair, put on his most charming smile and hurried to where they stood. "Can I help you?"

"Not yet." The man returned Garrett's smile. "I was just telling my daughters they might as well walk down the street to look around while I decide what I need and get some feed loaded up. We're new around here. I'm Mason Tripley and these are my daughters, Delores and Esther."

"Welcome to Sandy Lake. I'm Garrett Young, and I'd be happy to escort these young ladies around town if you'd like."

Mr. Tripley's brows went up, but before he could reply, a voice behind Garrett interrupted. "Garrett. I'd like to speak to you in the office."

Garrett jumped. How had his cousin sneaked up on him like that? Downright rude of him. Regardless, Garrett had no choice but to follow him to the office.

Irv kept his voice down because voices carried to the front even from here. His face was red, even his ears. Garrett had never seen him so angry. "What do you think you're doing? Offering to escort customers around town?"

Heat washed up Garrett's neck and cheeks. How dared Irv use that tone with him? He was family. "Just trying to be polite to the customers the way you're always telling me. Pretty rude of you to interrupt that way."

His cousin snorted—an unpleasant sound that rushed though his mouth and nostrils. His voice rose. "Being polite to the customers has *never* included escorting them around town."

"But these folks are newcomers. I thought you'd want me to give them special treatment so we'll be sure to get their business."

"Don't play your games with me, Garrett. I'm not your mother."

"I don't know what you're talking about. What does my mother have to do with this?"

"Your mother believes everything you tell her. I can see right through your tricks. The special treatment has *nothing* to do with hoping we get the newcomer's business and everything to do with the fact that the newcomers are female. Who's going to do your work while you're out gallivanting with the ladies?"

"You just don't trust..."

"I'm *so* disgusted with you, Garrett. This morning for the first time, I trusted you to open the store on your own. When I got here half an hour later, you still hadn't shown up." Irv paced in the narrow office, stirring up the dust that was inescapable at a mill.

"Who knows how many customers we lost during that time. When you finally waltz in, you play Don Juan, offering to escort women around town. I've half a mind to fire you."

Garrett's mouth hung open. His cousin never talked to him this way. What had gotten into him? Did he have indigestion or marriage problems?

He bit his tongue to keep from spewing out angry words. What could he say to soothe Irv's anger? Garrett's father had never whipped him but maybe this was how little boys felt after their first trip to the woodshed.

At last, his cousin stopped pacing. "I'm going to give you one more chance because you're family. That's the only reason. If you even *think* about lagging in here late again or pulling any other tricks like the one you pulled today, you're finished."

Irv spun around and marched in the direction of the Tripley's. Garrett's face burned, his fists clenched, his stomach churned. His cousin would be sorry.

CHAPTER 5

Polly woke the next morning with warm sunshine pouring through her window. Beth was already up and even Maggie's spot was empty. Tingles of dread unsettled her stomach as she threw back the covers. This morning she'd have to face her mother's disapproval. She groaned and buried her head in her pillow.

We went for a long ride in the country and lost all track of time. Or maybe.... *The weather was so beautiful. We didn't want the evening to end.* Those answers were true as far as they went.

Polly inched one leg over the edge of the bed, then the other, and forced herself to stand. It might help if the children hadn't left for school yet. She'd better hurry. She pulled on her dark blue work dress and pinned up her flyaway curls.

The children's voices echoed up the stairway from the dining room as she started down. Father would have had his breakfast long ago, but why wasn't Mother's voice calming the bedlam?

She started across the living room just in time to see Mother get up from the table and head for the kitchen, her hand clamped over her mouth. A door opened and closed.

"What's wrong with Mother?" Polly's brothers and sisters met her question with blank stares as she paused in the doorway.

"We don't know. She was fine a minute ago." Maggie stirred her oatmeal and turned a page in her book.

"Hurry up, Maggie." Ben looked at the clock. "We're going to be late for school."

As Maggie closed her book and Ben pushed past her, Polly took a few steps. She wanted to check on her mother but... *You are such a coward. You're old enough to stop feeling nauseous about whether or not Mother approves of everything you do.*

In spite of her brave words, pleasing her mother had been her life-long priority until Garrett came along. Now pleasing him was fighting for first place. She didn't want to give up her time with Garrett even if Mother didn't approve. Since graduating from high school, she didn't have much of a social life otherwise.

The back door opened and closed. Mother plodded into the dining room looking pale and weak. Polly ran to her side. "What's wrong? Are you sick?"

Mother gave a little warning shake of her head as she glanced at the younger children still seated at the table. "I'm all right." She clutched the back of a chair and then sank into it.

"Oh Mother, no..." Polly ignored the look in her mother's dark brown eyes. "Surely you aren't..."

"Florence."

When her mother used that voice, Polly swallowed the rest of her words.

"We'll talk about this later. Please help the little ones get washed up and clear the table. Beth, Robert, George, hurry and finish or you'll be late."

Polly got a washcloth and sponged Twila's sticky hands, then Elsie's. How many other times had her mother gotten sick at the breakfast table and refused to talk about it in front of the children? When Polly was younger, she'd always been sure her mother had a terrible disease and worried that she would die.

Now that she was older, her concerns were different. She gathered a load of dirty dishes and headed for the kitchen. Biting her lip, she pushed down her resentment at the changes that would come if she was right about the cause of her mother's behavior. It didn't seem fair—just when Mother had regained her strength and Polly had begun to have more freedom.

She poured hot water from the teakettle into the dishpan and blushed at how she'd been using that freedom with Garrett. *I'm so tired of feeling guilty about everything, especially when it comes to Garrett.*

"Maybe I've got it all wrong," she said aloud, scrubbing at the crusty oatmeal on the breakfast dishes. "Maybe it's not as bad as I think. Maybe Mother has a mild case of influenza."

Mother stuck her head in the doorway. "Who are you talking to?"

Polly flushed. "No one."

"Would you keep an eye on Twila and Elsie? I'm going upstairs to lie down for a while."

The only time Mother went upstairs to lie down was early in her pregnancies, but Polly had to try. "Are you *sure* there's going to be another baby? Are you sure you don't have influenza? I've heard there's a lot of it going around."

Rubbing her hands over her tired face, Mother's tall body slumped. "No, Polly, I'm not sure. After eight children, you'd think I *would* be sure. We'll have to wait and see. I'm sorry—I know it would make your life more difficult."

Compassion washed away Polly's rebellion. "I'm sorry to be such a grouch. It's just that sometimes..." Her voice trailed off.

"Sometimes you'd rather have more time for fun?" Mother smoothed down several strands of Polly's flyaway hair. "I understand, dear. But perhaps for some reason, that isn't what's best for you."

Polly grew still under Mother's hand. Had Father told her about the late hour Polly had gotten home last night? Would she get another lecture about Garrett and whether or not this was a serious relationship? But Mother only hugged her tight before turning toward the door. "Elsie and Twila are playing in the living room. Don't leave them alone too long."

The morning had not turned out the way she'd expected. Maybe it had been a blessing in disguise that Mother's morning sickness or influenza had begun today. She should be relieved. Instead, she wrestled a mixture of emotions. Maybe it would have been better to talk to her mother about what happened last night.

Polly picked up a dishtowel. She loved being with Garrett, she loved having a good time, and she loved having him tell her, as he had last night, how beautiful she was. Why else would she have let him kiss her with such passion and take such liberties?

She dashed in to check on Elsie and Twila. They didn't even notice her as they played with some of Mother's empty spools, so she returned to the kitchen.

Why hadn't she told her mother everything? If she had, Mother might not allow her to see Garrett anymore. She might have to choose between Mother or Garrett's approval. If she stopped allowing Garrett's passionate behavior, would she ever see him again? Chills of loneliness gnawed at the pit of her stomach. The fear of losing him was greater than her fear of her mother's disapproval.

With a deep sigh, Polly rinsed the dishcloth and dumped the dirty water down the drain. She couldn't risk talking to Mother about Garrett. She already disapproved of him. Her mother was nearly always right about everything, but this time, Polly hoped she was wrong.

Chapter 6

Margaret Dye labored up the stairs, pausing several times, waiting for her lightheadedness to clear. These steps had never seemed so steep or numerous, even on the day they moved in. She fought back tears. She'd been so hopeful about the future that day in spite of her weariness.

She climbed the last two steps. Just a few days ago, she'd been reveling in her family, her newfound strength, and the wonderful warmth of the sun on her face as she hung out baskets of fresh-smelling laundry. She'd felt almost invincible, able to take on the world, and undaunted by the mounds of dirty laundry produced by a family of ten.

Today, climbing the stairs to her bedroom seemed an insurmountable task. Margaret sighed and walked down the cool, dim hall, through the drab though sunlit nursery and into the bedroom she shared with her husband. Automatically, she stepped over the creaky board, pulled down the window blinds, and sat on the edge of the bed. She yawned. Sleep is what she needed.

Relaxing against her pillows, an odd foreboding, a darkness or oppression, sent prickles up her arms. She prided herself on her no-nonsense approach to life, so she had chosen to ignore this sensation she'd had several times. No matter how hard she tried, she couldn't deny its existence.

How can I scold Polly for letting her imagination run away with her when I can't control my own? Enough. I have more important things to think about. Was another little Dye on the way? Since she still nursed Twila, she hadn't been concerned about her monthly flow not starting... hadn't worried until today.

But her symptoms this morning were hard to ignore. "Forgive me, Father," she whispered to the One she knew always listened. "I don't know why I'm so upset. I know many women my age who have more children than I do and don't seem to mind at all. Maybe I'm upset because I know how Florence feels about it."

She took a deep breath. "Help me trust you regardless of whether or not I'm pregnant." She closed her eyes, relaxed her jaw and her tenseness drained away as His peace settled over her.

Florence... so full of life that it almost oozed out of her pores—even her red hair had a vitality all its own—and so compassionate and kind to anyone in need. What did the future hold for her firstborn, fast becoming a woman?

Garrett. She frowned and touched the two sharp lines that creased her forehead. "Father, I don't want to think ill of Garrett or displease you by unkind thoughts. Still, I don't trust him or his intentions. He appeals to Polly's fun-loving nature, but please protect her from being carried away by her emotions."

Turning on her side, Margaret nestled her head into her down-filled pillow. These problems were too big for her to handle. Experience had taught her that if she tried to solve things on her own, she would only make things worse. The only solution was to release her worries and revert to the childlike faith that had always sustained her. Her eyelids drooped and she smiled as the burdens slipped out of her hands.

♠

Downstairs on the floor of Mother's sitting room, Polly helped Elsie and Twila build a tower, then watched them knock it down. Her mind was still busy weighing the positives and negatives of talking to Mother about her evening with Garrett last night. She'd made up mind and then changed it more times than she could count.

I've been talking to Mother about nearly everything ever since the first grade when Willard tried to kiss me behind the schoolhouse. She helps me make the right decisions when life gets confusing. How can I be sure I'm doing the right thing if Mother doesn't approve?

Polly admired her mother's strong faith. Did she have an inside track with God? Sometimes disagreeing with Mother almost seemed like disagreeing with God, which made disagreeing with

Mother very scary. Polly didn't want to disagree with God. Well, at least not in principle.

Scooping up Twila to derail her thoughts, Polly kissed her soft cheek. "You're so beautiful, baby dear. Soon you won't be a baby anymore."

When had Twila lost some of her babyish plumpness and developed distinct features of her own? Polly had mourned a little when each of the younger children had left that baby stage, even though she'd known it meant less work for her. Did they have to grow up so fast?

Polly hummed a lullaby her mother had often sung. "Sleep, my child, and peace attend thee, all through the night." Twila's eyelids fluttered. "Guardian angels God will send thee, all through the night..."

Elsie still played contentedly, and Polly gave her a loving *I'll be right back* nudge with her toe as she tiptoed out of the room and up the stairs. She eased Twila into her crib outside her parents' door.

Maybe this would be a good time to talk to Mother...

Stop it. I got away with being out late last night without even a reprimand. Why would I consider bringing up the subject?

Polly opened the door to her parents' bedroom a few inches. *If Mother is awake, I'll talk to her and be done with it. I can't stand this indecision.*

Mother's back was turned making it impossible to tell if she was sleeping. Polly took a few steps into the room and peered at the floor. Where was the squeaky board? Blinking to adjust to the gloom, she noticed a definite indentation on the floor to her right. She squatted to get a better look. *Were those boards loose? Could there be something hidden there? Money? Jewels?*

Polly explored the board with her fingers and to her delight, a short section of floorboard came away in her hand revealing a small cavity between the floor and the ceiling below. She peered into the darkness and then reached gingerly into the hole. *What if mice or spiders made their home here?* She inched her fingers along until she came to the other side.

Empty.

No, wait—a flat object wedged against one side of the opening. She removed it, cobwebs and all. A book. She wondered how many years it had lain there. Blowing away a layer of dust from its faded cover, she peered at the raised letters—Diary? Spidery script covered the pages. Although it was impossible to read in the darkened room, she was sure it was a diary.

Polly hesitated and listened to her mother's even breathing. Completely unaware of the silent drama taking place a few feet from her bed, Mother slept.

Mother would never read someone else's diary. But how could Polly miss this opportunity of learning more about someone who had lived in this house? She might even find out if something had happened here to create the feelings of apprehension she'd had.

In one fluid movement, Polly leaned over and replaced the board. She had to read the diary. Later, she would decide whether to tell Mother. If necessary, she could simply put the diary back where she'd found it.

Polly carried the little book like buried treasure and hurried out of the room.

CHAPTER 7

Polly glided through the nursery and down the hall to her bedroom door. She paused. If Elsie weren't alone downstairs, Polly would have hidden herself away to satisfy her curiosity about the diary. She darted into her bedroom and slipped the tantalizing book in a drawer beneath some underwear. If Mother woke up before she had a chance to read it, it would be safe there.

Maybe if she hurried, she could give Elsie some lunch and get her down for a nap before Twila or Mother woke up. Polly flew down the steps.

A Child's Garden of Verses and *The Tale of Peter Rabbit* lay beside the davenport. Elsie had discarded them and pulled some of Mother's books from a shelf nearby. Polly took them with a gentle reprimand. "Those aren't children's books, Elsie. They belong to Mother."

Elsie scrunched her pretty face into a scowl. "Mine." Polly put the books back on the shelf, carefully arranged as Mother liked them, scooped Elsie up in her arms and headed for the kitchen. No use arguing with Elsie who could hold her own in any argument.

"Let's go find something to eat." Polly held the little girl close.

She worried sometimes that since Twila's birth, Elsie didn't get enough attention. Now with the possibility of a new baby, attention might be even harder to come by. She squeezed Elsie tighter and pressed kisses all over her rosy little face, and then shushed her when her high-pitched giggles rang out. "Don't wake Mother and Twila. They need some rest."

Boiled potatoes and cooked carrots from last night's dinner and some of the applesauce she had helped Mother can last summer would make a good lunch. She covered Elsie's pink cotton dress with a dishtowel while the food warmed on the stove. After checking the temperature, she started to put a spoonful of food into the little girl's mouth.

"Me do."

"All right." Polly gritted her teeth and handed Elsie the spoon before she could clamp her mouth shut and refuse to eat. The diary would have to wait.

"Pa-we, Elsie eat." Elsie put a dainty mouthful on her spoon and inched it toward her mouth.

"That's good, Elsie. But I think you can take bigger bites. At this rate, we'll still be eating lunch at suppertime."

Elsie giggled and took another tiny mouthful of food. "Elsie p'wite!"

Polly laughed at Elsie's imitation of their mother. "You can be polite with bigger bites."

At last Elsie had finished every bit of food, and Polly wielded the washcloth she'd grabbed.

"Elsie whoosh, pwease."

To avoid an argument, Polly held Elsie high in the air for a moment, then brought her down in a rush. "Time for a nap."

"No nap." Elsie stuck out her lip.

"We'll go for a walk and pick some flowers later if you're a good girl and don't fuss."

Elsie's face lit up, and Polly whisked her up the stairs, managing to avoid the creaky places. She shushed her several times and reminded her, "Whisper, Elsie," as she slipped her into her little bed across from Twila's crib. *Where will the new baby sleep—if there is a new baby? Perhaps Father will have to buy a double bed for Twila and Elsie.*

She kissed Elsie's freshly washed cheek and tucked the sheet around her. "Sleep tight, baby dear." It was a term she usually reserved for Twila but today, she wanted to do everything she could to make sure Elsie didn't grow up too soon.

"Night, Pa-we."

Twila didn't stir and no sound came from Mother's room even though Elsie's best effort to whisper was loud.

Polly put her finger to her lips and blew Elsie a kiss, then sped down the hall to her bedroom and shut the door. She blew out a big sigh of relief, curled up on the sunbathed double bed and opened the diary.

On the flyleaf she read, "This diary is the property of Sarah Davis, 1840." Polly hesitated, then shook her head. Her desire to know Sarah Davis, probably a former resident of this house, was too strong. The handwriting was a younger, firmer version of the spidery penmanship toward the back of the book.. She turned the page.

May 14, 1840. I was never much of a hand at writing or keeping a diary but now that Thomas and I are married, it seems like a good idea. Maybe it will help us remember important dates and occasions if the Lord grants us long life. I hope and pray He will see fit to do that as He has seen fit to bring us together. I can't doubt that His hand was on us—bringing Thomas all the way from Ireland to this little spot in Sheakleyville.

So Sarah Davis hadn't lived her whole life in Sandy Lake or in this house. Still, if Sarah had hidden the diary in the back bedroom, surely she had written a little about events that happened here. But maybe there *was* no connection between Sarah and the darkness in this house. Maybe her imagination was leading her astray again. Sarah's words sounded very much like something Polly's mother would have written.

What about other people in Sarah's family? She turned back to the diary.

Thomas is as kind a husband as any woman could want. He is a good provider, too, working hard at his trade.

Then there was Garrett with his many excuses for not going to work. She hurriedly read on.

He goes from farm to farm making shoes as needed—an ideal occupation for someone who loves to talk and share stories as he does, regaling his listeners with his famous "Paddy" humor which he inherited from his father. He is a welcome visitor at the farms not only for the fine shoes he produces but also for the laughter he brings. Even though his visits sometimes take longer than they should, how can I begrudge him the joy of friendship that is so necessary to his nature?

What a delightful fellow. If only she could have known him. Nothing to indicate he might be the kind of person to bring darkness into a home. Could it be the chill of apprehension was a premonition of bad things to come? She shivered and read on, determined to find that the cause was in the past, not the future.

July 27, 1840. I haven't done as well at writing in this journal as I had hoped. I guess it will still serve its purpose even if I only record special times. My body has been sending me messages for several months—messages I wouldn't allow myself to believe for fear of finding that my monthly was only late again. Today for the first time, I felt movement and life in my womb. Thomas will be so excited when he gets home. Even though he may hope for a boy, if God should give a girl, I will name her "Mary" after my mother. I hope this will be only the first of many children God will send to bless our home. I am excited but also fearful. There are so many diseases waiting to claim the innocent, and sometimes the offspring of those transplanted from Ireland are especially fragile. Only God could see me through the loss of a child.

Polly did the arithmetic. Sarah had lived 70 years ago in a more perilous world than she. Doctors would have been scarce and death a much more frequent visitor during that time. Now there were many more doctors with more remedies at their disposal, though death was still not an uncommon occurrence. Sarah didn't voice any concern for her own safety, only for that of her children. Childbirth itself was a significant risk in Sarah's day.

Dear Dr. Cooley had brought the last three little Dyes into the world. His kind words and encouraging manner were a comfort, even though none of the children had ever had serious illnesses. Polly shuddered. How awful to lose a child.

As if to allay her fears, Twila's lusty cries came from the nursery. Her volume always notified the household she'd had quite enough of napping. No chance she'd go back to sleep or that Elsie would sleep through this racket.

Polly slipped the diary reluctantly back under her cotton bloomers. Discovering more about Sarah and Thomas—and maybe more about this house—would have to wait.

CHAPTER 8

Polly reached for another juicy-looking tomato as the hot August sun beat mercilessly on her head. She pushed the damp strands of hair from her face, wet with perspiration.

"Why do we have to pick tomatoes when it's so hot?" George's whiney voice from the other end of the row grated on her nerves.

"Mother said they must be picked today before they rot on the vines."

"Let 'em rot." George's words were rebellious but quiet.

"If they rot, we won't have tomato juice or stewed tomatoes this winter." Canning in the hot kitchen, more work to add to the other chores that never stopped. Polly groaned. Mother should be here helping instead of at the WCTU meeting.

"How come Beth doesn't have to help?" George again. "It isn't fair." Always the expert on fairness, that boy.

"Mother says she's too little. She doesn't know which tomatoes are ripe. She'll get her turn soon enough when you boys are off working in the mines with Papa and Ben."

"I wish I were working in the mines today." George wiped his face on his large red handkerchief. "At least it would be cooler."

"Not me. I don't plan to ever go underground my whole life." Robert's jaw jutted in a stubborn line.

Polly hid a smile. "What *do* you plan to do when you grow up?"

"I don't care as long as it's above ground."

Polly waited for George to make a comment. He didn't disappoint her.

"That's just 'cause you're a 'fraidy cat."

"Am not."

"Are too."

It could be worse. Mother could be pregnant instead of just at a meeting. What a gray day when it had looked like she was pregnant again. But Papa had come down with a mild case of influenza the next day, followed by Maggie and Beth. The possibility of a different reason for her symptoms had lifted Mother's spirits. As soon as it ran its course, she regained the ground she'd lost.

I'm thankful for only two little ones to look after, not two with another one on the way. If Maggie hadn't volunteered to watch Elsie and Twila today, they would have been like two tornadoes in the tomato patch.

"Polly, Robert's picking green tomatoes."

"It was an accident. I didn't mean to."

"George, stop tattling." Polly stood up for a minute to stretch her muscles. "You'll soon have a reputation as a tattle tail."

Maggie might be watching Elsie and Twila, but I'm still in charge while Mother's away. I love my brothers and sisters, but honestly, sometimes I just get tired of being the mother.

Polly sighed. She shouldn't begrudge Mother going to a meeting now and then. It wasn't like she went often. By evening, her mother always looked tired.

Wiping the sweat from her forehead, Polly tuned out the boys' bickering. There hadn't been much time for reading Sarah's diary with all the summer work. The few minutes she'd managed to read, she hadn't found anything out of the ordinary—unless you called having three children in less than three years out of the ordinary. Maybe nothing bad had happened in this house. Maybe it had nothing to do with Sarah's family. Other people probably lived here, too.

If the diary couldn't explain the unexplainable in this house, she found it safer to assume—she paused and searched for words—the oppression, foreboding, she sensed at times had to do with other people who'd lived here rather than with things that were *going* to happen. Fear nibbled at her.

One of the children might be thrown from their buggy and run over by a horse-less chariot. Polly shuddered. Or Papa might be trapped in a cave-in at the mine. She closed her eyes—she never allowed herself to think about cave-ins. Mother might die in childbirth. Suddenly she couldn't breathe. Where had that awful possibility come from? Mother wasn't even pregnant. *Oh God, how would we survive?*

Polly plopped down on the ground fighting to catch her breath. God. Sarah's faith in God resonated in almost every entry. She reminded Polly so much of her own mother. They both depended on God for everything. Polly believed in God, but compared to Sarah and her mother, she was barely on speaking terms with Him. How had they developed such strong faith?

Was it the result of strong relationships with their husbands? Polly had always admired her parents' relationship, and Sarah's love and respect for Thomas shone through even mundane entries in her diary. Could Garrett ever be that kind of husband?

Surely Thomas wasn't perfect either. Maybe Sarah only wrote the good things. It wasn't fair to compare Garrett with someone she didn't even know.

Polly squirmed. Why did she make so many excuses for not comparing Garrett with men who were good husbands? She hadn't talked to Mother about her concerns the day she found the diary or any day since. *I'm almost 19 years old, old enough to make my own decisions.*

Just as summer chores hadn't left much time for reading, they hadn't left many opportunities for seeing Garrett either. It could be her imagination, but he hadn't seemed too disappointed the last couple times she'd been too busy to go out with him.

Straightening to rub her back again, Polly gasped. Garrett loped down the road with a fishing pole in his hand. "Garrett, why aren't you at work?"

"Too nice to be indoors. I'm going to the creek."

Tall trees shaded the brook just a quarter mile down the road. It sounded wonderful. "But didn't you say your cousin would fire you if you messed up again?"

"He won't find out. I'll tell him I was sick."

"But..."

"Don't start preaching at me about telling the truth. You sound just like your mother."

Polly gazed at Garrett, her stomach in knots at the ongoing conflict. She'd missed him and wanted to be with him. Why did they always end up fighting about something?

Before she could change her mind, she said, "Garrett, let me come with you. Robert and George can finish picking the tomatoes."

Ignoring the anguished yelps from her brothers, Polly started toward the road. But Garrett shook his head. "Not today, Pol. Today I need some time to myself. Maybe another day."

Polly stopped smiling and opened her mouth to argue, but Garrett strode away, his fishing pole at a rakish angle on his shoulder. She returned to the garden, ignoring her brothers, refusing to meet their eyes, humiliated more than she cared to admit by Garrett's brush off. Maybe he wanted to get even for all the times she'd told him no. He didn't understand they needed her at home.

Stealthily, Polly wiped a tear sliding down her hot face. She'd been so sure Garrett loved her, even though he didn't talk about marriage. If he did love her, why hadn't he let her go fishing with him? He'd never seemed the type to crave solitude. What if he was seeing someone else?

Squaring her shoulders, Polly took some deep breaths and went back to picking tomatoes. Mother would say she was overreacting. Nothing bad was going to happen to their family, and maybe Garrett did need time to himself. By the time she headed for the house, her bucket overflowing with tomatoes, she was humming under her breath.

♠

Whistling cheerfully, Garrett strode toward his destination. He didn't think Polly suspected anything in spite of the narrow escape. He wouldn't have planned to fish so near her house if he'd known she'd be in the garden. She was never available when he wanted her, maybe he should just break things off. Polly was still the prettiest girl he knew—but not the only one.

Garrett threw back his head, allowing the sun to beat on his face, basking in its warmth. He hadn't missed a single day of work or even been late since that day almost three months ago when Irv had bawled him out and threatened to fire him. Surely he had earned a day off to go fishing.

"And I aim to catch a nice one today." He grinned to himself.

Sprinting the last hundred yards of dusty road, Garrett veered off to the right just before he reached the narrow bridge that allowed travelers to cross the creek toward Greenville. He splashed some clear, cold water on his face from the brook that flowed over moss-covered rocks, then followed it into the cool, shaded woods.

When his eyes adjusted to the dim light of the forest, he thought he saw movement around the bend. "Yoo hoo," he called in a low tone and hurried to catch up. As he rounded the bend, Delores Tripley came into view, looking cool and delicious in her mint green summer frock.

"Hey, Pretty Lady." Closing the gap between them, he couldn't help comparing her to Polly, sweaty and hot in her drab, brown work dress. Surely no one could blame him for noticing things like that. Not that Polly wasn't a knock out when she dressed up.

He'd had a hard time convincing Delores nothing serious was going on between him and Polly. But though she had yet to agree to an outing in public, at least she'd consented to a secret meeting. That suited him fine. That way he could keep seeing Polly once in awhile. Garrett didn't mind seeing two girls at the same time. The secrecy made things more interesting. In fact, sometimes he thought three would be even better, though he'd yet to be *that* lucky.

Running the last couple steps, he held out his arms. Delores never quibbled about whether it was daytime or dark or any nonsense like that. As their lips met, Garrett thought about Delores' sister, Esther. Each of them was attractive in her own way. New in town, they were eager for dates. Maybe if he played his cards right, he could have them both.

CHAPTER 9

Garrett hummed as he strode down Mill Street. How could he help but be happy after such a good day of "fishing" yesterday? He chuckled. He'd told his mother Irv had given him the day off so a few of the summer help could have more hours before school started. She hadn't suspected a thing. His father, always gone early, would believe whatever Ma told him.

When the sun had streamed through his bedroom window this morning, he'd been tempted to take another day off, but he didn't want to push Irv too far. A slight breeze ruffled his hair and tingled against his clean-shaven face, just as Delores's soft cheek had the day before. Her blonde hair delighted him. Even so, he already had a few ideas about finding a way to date her sister. He loved a challenge.

If the sisters were competitive, Esther might welcome an opportunity to date him behind Delores' back. On the other hand, if they were the loyal type, he might end up losing both of them. He'd have to proceed with caution.

Both girls were beautiful. Delores so bubbly and bright with such fair skin that she had to be careful of the August sun, and Esther so dark and mysterious, with olive skin. Which one would be the best complement to his own good looks? Hard to know.

He took one more longing look at the sun before opening the side door of the mill. Stepping inside, he waited for his eyes to adjust to the dusty, dim light.

"Garrett, come to the office at once." His cousin had a nasty disposition.

Maybe he should've had his mother tell Irv he was sick yesterday, and then found a way to slip out of the house later. If Irv had known he wasn't coming in, they might have avoided any unpleasantness. After three months of perfect attendance, he hadn't thought Irv would fuss over just one day.

Garrett walked into the small, stuffy office with his most pleasant smile. "Morning, Irv. I'm sorry I was too sick to come to work yesterday. Ma was sick, too, or she could have told you I wouldn't be here."

Irv didn't smile. In fact, his face looked more like a storm cloud than like the sunny day Garrett had been enjoying. "Lay off, Garrett. I sent John over to your house yesterday. He saw you leaving with a fishing pole—"

"Around noon I felt better." Garrett shrugged. "I didn't want to come to work in case I might be infectious."

"Oh really? You didn't seem too concerned about Delores Tripley's welfare. But then, laziness and lying aren't generally contagious."

Garrett's face heated. His mouth fell open and he shut it with a snap.

"You... You... You've been spying on me? What a low-down, dirty, rotten trick."

Irv let out that high-pitched cackle he hated. "You would know more than anyone about low-down, dirty, rotten tricks. If you were trustworthy, I wouldn't have to send people to spy on you. I told you three months ago I'd given you your last warning, and I meant it. Family or not, you've run out of chances."

"You're firing me? You can't be serious. I'm your best salesman." Had the imbecile forgotten he'd had the highest sales of anyone last month?

"You are a good salesman—when you bother to show up. A dependable workman is more important to me than one with a silver tongue. And being reliable is something you know nothing about."

"You're making a big mistake." Garrett pointed his index finger at Irv. "If you fire me, I'll tell everyone in town how unfair you've been."

Laughing, Irv stood up. "I'll stake my word against yours in this town any day." He walked out of his office.

Garrett stood frozen, staring after Irv, his heart pounding and palms sweating. He could count on one hand the number of times he hadn't had the last word. With his charm, good looks and winsome tongue, he could talk his way out of any situation. How dare Irv fire him?

What to do now? He'd talk to his mom and dad, and they'd make Irv give back his job. But what if his father believed Irv's story instead of his?

He'd talk to all the farmers, their biggest customers, and get them to put pressure on Irv. He'd tell them if they helped him get his job back, he'd make sure they got better prices.

Still trying to make plans, Garrett tromped to the back door. Another day off didn't appeal to him as it had a few minutes ago, sunshine or not. Self-pity and revenge vied for center stage all the way home.

Ma, up to her elbows in hot, soapy water at the kitchen sink, looked up as he came in the back door. Her eyes widened. "What are you doing home already?"

He'd hoped she'd be out doing her marketing so he'd have more time to plan what to say. Everything seemed to be working against him today. He put on his saddest expression. "You'll never guess what Irv did."

"What now?"

She had her, *Why doesn't my cousin treat our son with the respect he deserves* look and he knew he was on the right track. "You know how he told me I could have the day off yesterday?"

"Yes, I thought that was nice of him." She dried her hands on a dishtowel.

"Well, today he fired me for not showing up."

"Fired you?" Ma's honest, blue eyes darkened. "I can't believe he'd treat a member of his own family that way."

"Believe it because that's exactly what he did."

"Of course I believe you, Son. It's just that I don't understand how he could be so unfair."

Garrett said nothing as his mother wiped a few tears with the dishtowel. Maybe he could still benefit from his cousin's actions. He put his arm around his mother's shoulders. "Ma, I have an idea."

His mother's face brightened. She'd do almost anything to cheer him up. "Remember how I've talked about wanting to buy a car? If I had a car, I could get a job in another town that might pay more than Irv is willing to pay anyway. In no time, I could probably earn enough to repay you and Pa every cent it would cost you."

A doubtful frown wrinkled his mother's forehead and Garrett hurried on. "I just can't work for Irv anymore. He has a grudge against me. He's unreasonable and demanding. I'd be better off somewhere else."

"Isn't there anywhere in Sandy Lake you could get a job?"

"You know how small towns are. Everyone will soon know Irv fired me. Who'll want to hire me then?"

"Son, I don't know. You know how your father feels about those 'horseless chariots.' He's hated them ever since that Steamer car roared down Main Street and spooked his horse years ago."

Garrett looked down.

"But I'll see what I can do." At the urgency in her voice, he looked up again with hope-filled eyes.

She patted his back. "Maybe a car is just what you need to get a fresh start in another town."

CHAPTER 10

Worn burgundy diary in hand, Polly sat down and leaned against the tree that shaded the front porch. She wanted to learn more about the journal's author and perhaps the history of their house, but she also wanted to enjoy these fleeting October moments of Indian summer. Mother still didn't know about the diary but if necessary, she'd say it was a book she'd found.

June 25, 1847. I've sadly neglected recording events in this little book since the birth of our sweet Nancy three years ago in June. I'm so filled with sorrow it's hard even to think about putting into words the entry I must make.

Polly trembled at the foreboding words but forced herself to read on.

Nancy's entry into the world was difficult, and my every waking moment was consumed with fighting a fierce battle with the grim enemy that has robbed so many women of their young. Sleep was a rare luxury I could seldom afford. With Mary and Elizabeth still hardly more than babies, I was never idle long enough to do more than note Nancy's birth in this journal during those three traumatic years

Ever since the early cold spell in September had forced them to spend more time indoors, Polly had dwelt more on the apprehensive feeling she'd had when they'd moved in, a feeling she still occasionally battled. Canning had occupied her time and her hands, but not her fertile imagination. Today perhaps she would discover something concrete to substitute for all the fantasies she had spun.

Yesterday the battle was finally over. Our little Nancy is now safe in the arms of Jesus. Even as I make that statement, part of me wants to rail against God because, though we have two other children, my arms are so empty. Is this how the disciples felt when Jesus asked them if they would leave Him, too, when many others had stopped following Him? They said, "Lord, to whom else shall we go?" If I turn against God, to whom will I go for comfort and strength to get through the days ahead? My beloved Thomas is struggling so desperately that I dare not lean too heavily on his meager strength.

Polly blinked to rid her eyes of the tears that blurred them. Sarah's other two children might have been close to the ages of Elsie and Twila. It must have been so hard for Sarah to look after their needs in the midst of her sorrow. Wiping her tears on her sleeve, Polly read on.

Although it's difficult to look after Mary and Elizabeth, I can't allow well-meaning family members to relieve me of their care even for a few days. In spite of the fact I was unable to protect Nancy in the final battle, my fear of something befalling the other two is very strong. I know it's unreasonable to believe they're safer with me than with anyone else but perhaps fear has nothing to do with reality.

While Polly's experiences with death had been limited to distant relatives, she could identify with Sarah's fear. She sometimes sensed an inner resistance to allowing Maggie or Ben to be in charge when Mother was away, as though she could prevent something bad from happening by remaining in control. So far, nothing had happened to challenge that assumption.

She turned a page hoping for something more positive.

Even in all this, I see God's hand of mercy because the child that moves in my womb gives me hope and a reason to go on. If our great sorrow doesn't hasten the process, this child should be born in about a month and a half. Thomas and I have decided if it's a girl, we'll name her Nancy in honor of her little sister in heaven. Not that anyone could ever take her place, but God's timing is no accident. I'm trying hard to say with Job, who suffered losses I can't even comprehend, "The Lord gave and the Lord hath taken away; blessed be the name of the Lord."

Polly snapped the book shut. How could anyone say, "The Lord gave and the Lord hath taken away; blessed be the name of the Lord" after the death of a loved one? Her stomach churned. If God was good as her mother claimed, why would He allow something so precious to be taken from someone like Sarah, a woman who reminded Polly so much of her own mother?

She wanted to run to Mother and ask, no *demand*, an explanation. But how could she talk to her mother about this without telling her about the diary?

Strong emotions stole her breath as she sat beneath the maple tree provided by her Creator. Her interest in Sarah was deeper than an effort to dispel her curiosity about the house. Sarah had become a real person with whom, for some reason, Polly identified very deeply. Why did she care so much about Sarah's loss?

Suddenly she sat up straight and clasped her hands. It wasn't Sarah's loss she cared about. Sarah's life was over; nothing could touch her. The heart of the matter was that if God would allow something precious to be taken from Sarah who was so devoted to God, then He might also allow something precious to be taken from Polly's mother or even from Polly herself.

Absentmindedly, she gathered the red, gold, and green leaves that had floated down from the maple tree. Every year, she clung to the warmth of summer, defying fall and winter to rob her of the beauty of these golden days.

She needed to focus on something good to lift her spirits as Mother always encouraged her to do. Garrett. Her lips twitched. Mother's face would be a thundercloud if Polly said taking her advice had prompted her to think about Garrett. Mother might not agree that such thoughts qualified as good. Still, there was no doubt that at his best, he lifted Polly's spirits.

Garrett had told her finding a job would take up most of his time so she'd seen very little of him. Not that she'd have been available anyway. Did her parents know about his job loss? *She* hadn't told them, but one never knew what they might hear at the market or the post office. If they heard, what effect would it have on their image of Garrett?

Not all thoughts of Garrett were uplifting, so she deliberately focused on their buggy rides, his passionate kisses and the sweet things he whispered in her ear. When the canning was done and Garrett got another job, maybe they could talk of marriage.

She leaned her head against the maple tree. Someday, Garrett would take her hand, look deep into her eyes, and say, "Polly, surely you must know I love you more than life itself. Will you do me the honor of being my wife?"

Then he'd put a sparkling diamond ring on her finger—Polly couldn't decide exactly what sort of ring it would be—and kiss her until it took her breath away. Later she would take his breath away, a vision of loveliness in the finest wedding gown imaginable, with a long train covered with lace. And always, they would be blissfully happy ever after.

Several quick gunshots shattered the peaceful afternoon. A shiny black car careened toward her. Not gunshots but a car backfiring. Who was at the wheel? She shaded her eyes. Doc Cooley, who had bought the first gasoline-powered automobile in Sandy Lake last year, wouldn't drive that fast.

The car lurched to the right. She scrambled to her feet when it headed straight for her, the diary tumbling to the ground. At the last possible minute, the driver straightened the wheels of the shiny Model T Ford and stopped on the other side of the tree. Polly's jaw dropped when Garrett opened the driver's side door and slid out.

CHAPTER 11

"Where did... What are... I mean—" Polly tripped over the diary, pupils dilated, as she stumbled toward the car.

Garrett, his face wreathed in smiles, sprang out and lovingly polished the windshield with his sleeve before joining her on the bank. "How do you like my new car?"

Polly's mouth dropped open. "This is *your* car?"

"Doesn't belong to anyone else."

"But you're not even working are you?"

"No, but this beauty will help me get a job. It'll take me wherever I need to go. Wanna go for a spin?"

Polly sighed. Nothing was ever simple. Part of her wanted to jump in the car and go off with Garrett without a second thought, but... "I'd better talk to Mother first."

"You're nineteen years old. When are you going to grow up?"

"I'm surprised you even know I'm nineteen since you didn't say a word about my birthday last month." Polly glared at him.

Garrett shrugged and avoided her eyes. "Don't change the subject."

"It's almost time to start supper. Mother might need help with the girls."

"You could bring them with you."

Polly stared at Garrett, eyes wide. He must be desperate to show off his new car because he'd never suggested taking Twila and Elsie with them. She hesitated, then remembered Garrett's recklessness. "No. No, I don't think so. They're so little. They might be frightened by the noise."

"Florence, are you all right?"

Polly turned and took a few steps to the left so her long skirt concealed the diary. Mother stood in the doorway a frown wrinkling her brow.

"I heard a lot of noise." Mother's gaze flicked to Garrett and her frown deepened.

"I'm fine. Garrett just stopped to show me his new Model T. Isn't it wonderful?"

Mother looked doubtful as she glanced at the vehicle. "I suppose your Father would think so. I still prefer horses and buggies myself."

"Do you think I could go for a quick ride or are you ready to start supper?"

Mother compressed her lips—a sure sign she wanted to say no. Finally, coming to the edge of the porch, she stared at Garrett. "How long have you been driving this horseless chariot? Do you know what you're doing?"

Garrett scowled as he often did when he and Mother talked. "Course I know what I'm doing. It's my car."

"How long?" Mother's tone brooked no avoidance.

Above the collar of Garrett's pale blue shirt, a red flush crept up his neck—something Polly had only seen once or twice before.

"Never mind. I can tell you're looking for reasons to forbid Polly to go with me. There are plenty of girls whose mothers won't mind letting them ride in my car."

"Young man—"

Garrett jumped into his shiny car and slammed the door behind him. A minute later, he climbed out, his face flaming. He grasped the crank with his right hand.

Polly bit her lip. She'd heard if you used the wrong hand to turn the crank, you could break your thumb or your wrist. Garrett gave a quick twist. The car backfired, and he yanked his hand away and stuck his thumb in his mouth. His brows knit in concentration.

Feeling much younger than her nineteen years, Polly stood by the maple tree, first on one foot and then the other. She hated the familiar feeling of being torn between loyalty to her mother and her desire to please Garrett. Mother had gone back inside. As far as she was concerned, Garrett's rudeness had ended the discussion and any possibility of Polly going with him.

Polly chewed a fingernail. He'd said plenty of girls would be allowed to ride with him. Were they the reason she hadn't seen him lately? Of course she and Garrett weren't officially engaged, but it would only be a matter of time until he asked her to marry him, wouldn't it? Fear of losing him if she allowed Mother to dictate her decisions nibbled at her.

With one quick movement, Polly picked up the diary and dropped it into a deep pocket of her work dress. She edged closer to Garrett as he pulled on the cantankerous crank with his left hand, his cotton shirt soaked with sweat. She was afraid to ask if he was seeing someone else. Sometimes it was better not to know.

Just as the car roared to life, Polly yelled, "Garrett," but the engine drowned out her words. She couldn't let him go without her. In two long strides, Garrett opened the driver's door and leaped into the car as Polly opened the passenger's side. "Garrett, I'm coming with you."

Almost before the doors closed, Garrett let out the clutch and headed down the road, his jaw still clenched. Polly peered back at the house through clouds of dust. Had Mother seen them leave? The exhilaration of this new experience momentarily alleviated her guilt.

As they sailed across the little bridge, it shuttered and swayed. Obviously it had not been built with horseless carriages in mind. How fast were they going? If she asked, Garrett would think she was criticizing his driving.

The wild ride suited Polly's love of adventure, but she became uneasy as they gathered speed. She'd heard about accidents where cars collided with horses and buggies on the narrow, bumpy roads.

Polly glanced at Garrett. Should she suggest he slow down? Much as he had wanted a companion, he acted as if he'd forgotten she was there. He made a handsome picture, his hair blowing in the wind, his face a deep shade of bronze from the hours he'd spent in the sun.

Garrett turned to look at her, his scowl replaced by a glow of excitement and something else that Polly couldn't decipher. He reached out to touch her hand. "How do you like it?"

"It's grand." Polly squeezed Garrett's fingers. "But do you think we ought to slow down?"

Garrett jerked his hand away. "Just when I think you aren't as much like your mother as I'd imagined, you make a comment that sounds just like her. I didn't bring you along to tell me how to drive."

"I'm not criticizing, Garrett. I like going fast, but I'm afraid someone might get hurt if we meet a horse and buggy at this speed."

He scowled again and the corners of his mouth turned down. Would she ever understand his kaleidoscope moods?

♠

Garrett pulled on the accelerator lever, ignoring Polly's quick intake of breath. Why had he chosen her to be the first girl to ride in his new car when he could have asked Delores or Esther? They both loved being with him while it was clear Polly and her mother did *not* appreciate him. Perhaps Polly, in spite of her good looks, wasn't worth his time.

CHAPTER 12

Garrett pulled away with a loud squeal of tires. Polly climbed the porch steps, shoulders slumped, head drooping. The ride with Garrett wasn't worth the reprimand she knew she'd earned. The guilt she'd held at bay in the midst of her excitement flooded back. *Why did I go with Garrett after the way he treated Mother?*

Did she become a different person when Garrett was around? Or did he bring out a part of her she'd always repressed? She'd read a book about a girl who sometimes felt like she had a "terrible twin." Polly was beginning to understand what she meant.

She plodded across the front porch and inched open the screen door. Before Garrett had arrived, she'd been delighting in the warm weather. Soon it would be cold and all the doors would have to be closed. Polly shuddered. The unsettling feeling that lingered in the house seemed worse when all the doors and windows were shut.

Trying to shake off her fit of melancholy, Polly straightened her shoulders, lifted her chin and headed for the kitchen. Twila and Elsie's childish voices intermingled with the sound of Mother preparing supper. The smell of beef stew was in the air. Might as well go in and face the music. No sense in postponing the inevitable.

Mother looked up as she entered the kitchen. Polly opened her mouth to apologize, and then closed it. Maybe Mother hadn't even noticed she'd been gone. Maybe she just thought Polly had been outside under the tree. She covered her mouth and gave a gentle cough, swallowing the words she'd intended to speak. "Do you need help?"

She tried to read the expression in her mother's eyes while avoiding direct eye contact. Mother spoke slowly, her brown eyes stern. She stopped stirring as she enunciated each word. "Florence, deception can be accomplished just as much by silence as by words."

Polly's fragile defenses shattered. She threw her arms around her mother's neck and wept out all the tangled emotions and frustrations that had been building ever since she and Garrett started dating. Twila and Elsie tugged at her skirt.

"Oh, Mother, I'm so sorry. I know I shouldn't have gone with Garrett. I got scared when he said there were plenty of other girls whose mothers would let them ride with him. He's the only boy I really care about, and I don't want to lose him."

♠

Margaret stroked her daughter's luxurious red hair, tucking in some of the flyaway strands that always escaped. She reassured the wide-eyed little girls who had seldom seen their big sister cry. "Florence is all right."

"Do you know why I didn't want you to get involved with Garrett, Little One?" She tipped Florence's chin so she could look into her eyes. "Garrett's parents tried for years to have a child but were unsuccessful. When Garrett came along, his parents and grandparents doted on him. They thought he could do no wrong."

Patting her daughter's cheek, Margaret shook her head. "They gave him everything he wanted, and he grew up believing that's how life should be." She shook her head. "Whoever marries him will have an overgrown child on their hands because he's never matured. I don't want that for you."

"But I really believe I love him. I think about him all the time, even when I don't see him for days. Isn't that what love is like?" Florence gazed down at Twila, now clinging to her leg.

Margaret was silent for a moment. "Thinking about someone all the time is often part of love, but it's so much more than that. Love is respect, trust, and treating the other person the way we want to be treated. Does your relationship with Garrett contain those qualities?"

♠

Polly patted Twila's head and dug in her pocket for a handkerchief, snatching her hand away when she touched the diary. She took the clean hanky Mother pulled out of her own pocket, blew her nose and wiped her eyes. She was stalling. Her attraction to Garrett had nothing to do with the qualities Mother mentioned. Their relationship was mainly physical—her response to his good looks and his passionate kisses.

Physical attraction is important.

Her face flushed and she avoided Mother's eyes, looking instead at Twila who had plopped down at her feet. Looking up at last, she met her mother's gaze. "Isn't it important that I'm attracted to Garrett, that I have strong feelings for him?"

Mother took on a faraway look, the look she always got when she was praying for wisdom. When she spoke, her words were slow. "Of course attraction and feelings are important, but they can change quickly—especially when you find yourself living with a child in a grown up's body."

Ironic that Garrett had asked her earlier today when *she* was going to grow up. Now Mother implied *he* had a problem in that area. Why did life have to be so complicated? Why couldn't she have fallen in love with someone who measured up to Mother's standards?

What about your standards?

"Up, Pa-we." Stooping, Polly pulled Twila's plump, little body to her and began to cover her face with kisses. Then she gathered Elsie close as well. At least with her little sisters, she could give hugs and kisses without feeling guilty.

Polly didn't doubt that her parents loved her, but sometimes she felt left out when they were snuggling her younger sisters. She craved the kind of touching Garrett gave her when they weren't arguing. Was that the reason she was so afraid of losing him? Surely in time if they were on their own without any interference from grown-ups, the arguing would stop.

Instead of offering to help Mother with supper, she plopped down on the floor, joining her little sisters in their world. Wouldn't it be great to be a child again? But she and Garrett weren't children. What was it her mother had said? "Feelings can change quickly when you find yourself living with a child in a grown-up's body."

CHAPTER 13

The golden days of Indian summer had passed and although life was still busy, compared with the previous level of activity, the days dragged. The necessity of keeping doors and windows closed brought with it a downward plunge in Polly's spirits, made more intense by the fact that Garrett hadn't been back since the day he left in a huff. She wrestled with rumors that he was escorting the Tripley girls in his new car. He was probably being kind because they were new in town.

Polly prowled around the quiet house looking for something to do. She picked up Maggie's book and put it down. The older children were in school, Elsie and Twila napping, and Mother resting too—a rare occasion. There was always housework to do, but she didn't see anything that motivated her. At last, she climbed the stairs and flung herself on her bed. Life had lost its sparkle.

She plopped her pillow on top of her sister's and discovered the faded little diary she'd hidden there last week. She chewed her lip. Although reading Sarah's last entry had been uncomfortable, the journal still fascinated her. Unanswered questions about this house plagued her, as well as the apprehension that had become an almost constant companion. She picked up the book with her fingertips. Averting her eyes, she skipped over the last entry and began again.

August 1847. Well, our dear little Nancy was born last week, the picture of health—no evidence my grieving and fears affected her at all, at least not physically. I suppose it's too soon to tell whether it has affected her mentally or emotionally. What a comfort she is. Thomas and I can't get enough of holding her, and Mary and

Elizabeth seem to love their little sister. I keep them all very close because our loss is so fresh, and I don't think I could bear it if something should happen to any of them.

I just reread what I've written—what a faithless statement. I know if anything happens, God will be faithful to see us through.

Polly tensed. How could Sarah refer to God as "faithful" when He had allowed her precious baby to be taken? The next several entries were joyful birth announcements as Sarah gave birth to a son, Robert J., in 1848 and then in quick succession, two girls and another boy from 1849 to 1853, Sarah Lucinda, Naomi, and William.

As Sarah's entries portrayed uneventful life in the Davis household, Polly relaxed. Uneventful was preferable to tragedy. As she turned the page, Sarah's handwriting became shaky as it had been in the entry she'd read last week. She wanted to close the book and run, but some inner instinct compelled her to read on.

April 1855. Ever since our first little Nancy died in her third year, I've suffered anxiety when one of our children approaches the age of three. However, when Robert and Lucinda each completed that year, my anxiety for Naomi lessened. Then, last week less than two months after her third birthday, all my worst fears were realized. We'd heard that scarlet fever struck down several in our area. I should never have risked taking the little ones to church, but it was Easter Sunday and I did so want to celebrate the resurrection of our Lord. Three days later Thomas had to make yet another tiny coffin.

I don't know whether I will ever be able to forgive myself for having allowed Naomi to be exposed, although I'll never know for sure where she contacted the lethal disease. How could I have let down my guard? Thank God none of the other children came down with the fever, and yet again He has provided that as we face this loss, we have the promise of a new life already stirring in my womb. We haven't decided on a name.

Did we make a mistake giving our second Nancy the same name as the child we lost? Sometimes there's a darkening of her spirit that's abnormal for a child so young. Or perhaps it's only that I'm so attentive to her every mood and movement. I think I'm going to ask Thomas if we can move into one of the other properties he's purchased in Sheakleyville. This house simply has too many haunting memories.

With a sound somewhere between a sob and a snort, Polly dropped the book into her lap. Every fiber of her being resisted the knowledge that such heartache could come upon someone like Sarah. She'd known people who had suffered tragedies, but had always convinced herself they'd done something wrong or hadn't *truly* loved God. None of those definitions fit Sarah Davis.

How could Sarah continue to give thanks to God for things like the other children not getting scarlet fever and the new life in her womb? Couldn't she see that God had failed her, proving He wasn't faithful and couldn't be trusted?

Polly flung the diary on her bed, rushed out of her room, through the nursery where her sisters still napped and into her parents' bedroom. She stood beside her mother's prone form in the darkened room, willing her to open her eyes. At last Mother stirred and looked at Polly.

She sat upright. "What is it, Florence? Is something wrong with the girls?"

"Nothing's wrong with the girls, but I need you." Now that she had her mother's undivided attention, Polly didn't know what to say.

Mother pulled her pillows against the headboard and leaned back, her dark eyes never leaving her daughter's face. "Sit down, Florence." She patted the edge of the bed.

Polly sat, keeping her backbone ramrod straight. "Mother, why does God let bad things happen to good people—I mean, not just good *people* but good *Christians?*" She brushed a strand of hair out of her eyes. "How can you say He's faithful and good when He allows bad things to happen?"

"What raised such serious doubts in your mind?" Mother's brown eyes darkened. "What happened?"

"Nothing happened. Just a book I'm reading."

After a long, thoughtful pause, Mother took Polly's hand. "Florence, God never promised that things would go well for us if we loved Him and obeyed Him. In fact, we're told just the opposite."

Polly's eyebrows lifted, as Mother patted her hand. "Scripture says, *Many are the afflictions of the righteous*, and *In the* *world ye **shall have** tribulation.* But God does promise to go through trials with us and give us the strength we need."

Polly frowned and withdrew her hand.

"As for saying that God is faithful and good, those qualities are part of God's character. We evaluate all that happens in light of those qualities, rather than evaluating God's character in light of what happens to us." She smiled. "He remains faithful, good, just, kind and sovereign no matter what we're facing."

"What does 'sovereign' mean?"

"It means God is ultimately in control of what happens in our lives. It's the reason He's able to keep His promise in Romans 8:28 that 'all things work together for good to those who love God and are called according to His purpose'." She reached out to take Polly's hand again. "While He may not prevent bad things from happening, He promises to bring good from them."

"How can God possibly bring good from someone losing something precious to them?"

Mother leaned over and stroked her daughter's cheek. "It's a matter of trust, dear," she said gently. "It's a matter of trust."

CHAPTER 14

Garrett gave one last twist to the crank of his car and thrilled to the sound as it roared to life. The engine's power vibrated beneath his fingertips. Waving to his mother who stood watching in the doorway, he jumped into the driver's seat and headed down the road that led out of town.

He'd been "looking for work" for three weeks without success, which in no way dampened his enthusiasm for the process. He pulled down on the gas lever, loving the feeling of putting miles between himself and anyone who knew what he was supposed to be doing. He loved exploring new towns to discover anything or anyone who might prove interesting.

Pushing on the brake as he neared a narrow, bumpy stretch, Garrett prided himself on being quite skillful behind the wheel. Of course, there'd been a few *other* bumps in the road lately. His father was growing impatient with his lack of results.

"Garrett, do you have any possibilities for a job yet?" His *father had looked at him over the evening paper.*

"Not yet. But I'm looking every day."

"I'd hoped you'd soon start paying for the gas you're using. I thought that was our agreement."

Garrett pulled a sad face in his mother's direction.

"Now Abe, you know Garrett feels bad enough about not having a job. Don't be so hard on him."

Outnumbered again, his father had withdrawn behind his newspaper.

Garrett glanced at the falling autumn leaves, glad his father hadn't questioned him too closely about these excursions since his actual efforts to find work had been minimal. If he found a job, these daily jaunts would end.

He yanked down on the gas lever again as he glided on to a smooth patch of road, reveling in the power at his fingertips. Garrett rarely bothered to ask if any of the businesses he passed were hiring. He did stop one day when he'd seen a *help wanted* sign in a shop window but decided the pay wasn't enough to make it worthwhile. With few regrets, his "search" continued.

The best part of these job-hunting expeditions was the opportunity to meet some of the most fetching young women imaginable. Often Garrett would park his car and stroll up and down the streets, keeping a sharp lookout for anyone who might catch his eye. Nearly always, he found someone who met one of his criteria: a pretty or unusual face, a shapely figure, or some particularly outstanding quality. Today proved no exception.

As he began his Main Street strut in Jackson Center, a girl with hair the shade of deepest midnight and creamy skin with a tinge of rose on her cheeks came out of the hat shop across the street. Although Garrett was usually hesitant to approach the first pretty face he saw lest he see a prettier one later, he couldn't let this one get away. She had a magnetic quality that drew him across the street at an undignified trot. Just as he reached her side, she stepped down from the wooden sidewalk onto the dusty road.

Perfect timing. Garrett approached her and offered his arm. "Allow me to assist you in crossing the street, Miss."

♠

Maxwell Sullivan looked out his window in time to see Savannah Stevens gazing out the door of the hat shop. He watched as she reached the street just as the good-looking young man arrived at her side. *I bet she didn't miss a single detail of that nicely dressed fellow climbing out of his shiny Model T.*

The man was obviously a newcomer in town who knew nothing of Savannah's reputation. The poor kid had no way of knowing she'd seen the look on his face on the faces of other young men many times and was an expert at manipulation. What was her agenda this time? The bell on his counter jingled and Maxwell shook his head and turned away.

♠

Pulse racing, Garrett gazed at this lovely creature. Warmth spread through his chest as her fragrance permeated his nostrils. He searched his mind for a reason to get to know her. His usually silver tongue tripped over itself. "I want you to introduce me... I mean, you want me to introduce... I mean..."

Eyes the deepest shade of violet blue he'd ever seen turned toward him, and the young woman answered in a voice like thick, flowing honey. "Why aren't you the sweetest thing I've ever seen."

As fragile and defenseless as a tiny forget-me-not beside the path, she tucked her beautifully shaped hand with its faintly tinted nails into the crook of his arm and leaned against him. Her nearness scrambled his thoughts, and Garrett couldn't remember the usual line that worked so well with the young women he'd met in other towns. None of them were anything like this.

One small hand covered her mouth as a girlish giggle escaped. "I'm Savannah Stevens from Georgia." Her long lashes covered her magnificent eyes for a moment before she tilted her head to give him the full effect and added, "And who might you be?"

"Garrett." He couldn't look away from her face. "Garrett Young. And you are the most beautiful creature I've ever laid eyes on."

Savannah's laugh surrounded them and she clutched his arm tighter and leaned into him. "You're not too hard on the eyes yourself." Her gaze swept his face and travelled down to his shoes.

Heat rose to Garrett's neck and cheeks. He'd never had a woman look at him with such frank admiration. However, he recovered quickly. Why shouldn't a woman let a man know how she felt?

Patting her hand on his arm, he looked into Savannah's eyes. "Now that we've been properly introduced, I wonder if you'd accompany me to the inn on the corner that advertises hot breakfasts?" Although Garrett's mother had served him an enormous breakfast, he could think of no other excuse to remain in the presence of this fascinating woman.

"Why, honey, I just don't know—" Savannah hesitated but didn't relax her grip on his arm. "I hardly know you, and I don't know what folks would think."

As Garrett held his breath, Savannah gave him a dazzling smile revealing perfect white teeth.

"Oh, who cares what anyone thinks. I'm sure a gentleman like you must be completely trustworthy."

Garrett let out the breath he'd been holding as he steered her in the direction of the inn.

"By the way, what are you doing in town, stranger? Do you live far from here?" Savannah continued to look into Garrett's eyes as though she couldn't bear to miss a word he said.

"Actually, I'm looking for work." Suddenly finding a job in this town seemed essential. "Do you know if anyone is hiring?"

Savannah hesitated and played with the clasp of her bag "No," she said at last. "I don't think there are any jobs here. But there's a little town just a few miles away that might have something for you. What sort of job do you want?"

"I used to sell feed for my cousin at a gristmill, but I could probably sell just about anything. I was my cousin's best salesman."

They had reached the door of the inn and Savannah lifted her head. "I bet you were a good salesman, honey. I just bet you were. I know a man in Mercer that could probably use someone like you in his clothing store. Having you wear his clothes would be the best advertisement his money could buy. You just leave it to me, honey. Don't you worry about a thing."

CHAPTER 15

Snow glistened on the trees and houses and made large cupcakes out of shrubs and bushes as Polly walked down Broad Street. She shivered, shoving her mittened hands deeper into the pockets of her heavy winter coat, grateful for its warmth although she'd resisted wearing it. Each year she and her mother waged war before Polly yielded to her pleas to dress for winter.

Her size 6 boots slowed her pace and made footprints in the snow. She'd always hated wearing winter garments because they inhibited her freedom, but this year there was something more. Why was she fighting the passing of time? She couldn't bear to acknowledge one more day had passed, let alone accept the turning of each page on the Mercer County State Bank calendar that hung on the kitchen wall. It didn't make sense.

Polly stopped abruptly. The clip clop of horses' hoofs told her she'd reached Main Street. If she didn't pay attention, the horses and buggies would flatten her.

She sighed. Although she was usually happy for a reason to go somewhere, today she'd fussed when Mother asked her to go to the meat market. What was the use of going to town if there was no chance of seeing Garrett? She hadn't seen him for days. Someone said he'd gotten a job in Mercer. Shoulders slumped, she kept her eyes to the ground as she trudged through the snowy plank sidewalks.

Her mother was probably relieved Garrett wasn't coming around any more. Polly hadn't mentioned his absence. She was afraid Mother might say something disgustingly cheerful when all

Polly wanted was sympathy. Not that her mother was usually insensitive—except where Garrett was concerned.

Even Maggie had become insufferably self-righteous when Polly tried to talk to her about Garrett's absence. "Mother tried to warn you." Like *Maggie* always listened to everything Mother said.

"Hi Polly." The cheery voice belonged to their neighbor, Kitt Potter, who was just a few years older than Polly. She lived in a house on Broad Street that was more like a mansion. Polly gave a faint smile and waved back without a break in her disheartened thoughts.

Sometimes it was hard not to resent the freedom Maggie enjoyed in spite of the fact that they were only two years apart in age. Polly would have more free time if her sister took on some of her chores. Like that would happen as long as Maggie was in school.

Oh well, what would I do with more free time? Now that Garrett isn't around, I don't know what to do with the free time I have. After I help take care of the little ones, clean the house and cook, about all I do is read that old diary.

That was all the encouragement she needed to wander into Sarah's world. Even though it wasn't enormously exciting, losing herself in someone else's life helped ease her loneliness. In the last entries she'd read since Naomi's death, another son had been born, Richard Vance. On his fourth birthday, Sarah wrote joyously that he had successfully negotiated his third year—an answer to her prayers.

Almost 12 years without a death in Sarah's family. Were Sarah and Thomas's troubles over? But if they were, would her questions about the oppression in the Dye home be unanswered?

Polly stopped. She had passed the market completely and was headed up the street toward Jackson Center. What was the matter with her? If she didn't return to the real world, someone would take her to the madhouse. What would her friends think if they knew what a witless creature she had become?

Polly probably had only herself to blame for her loneliness. She'd become so obsessed with Garrett that she hadn't been a very good friend. She'd just passed Kitt without even speaking to her. Maybe she'd run into her at the market.

A car backfired as it came down the hill she'd almost needlessly climbed.

Garrett's car.

She raised her arm to wave, then dropped it. Seated beside him—no, *snuggled* against him, was the most stunning young woman Polly had ever seen. Even through the windshield, it was impossible to miss her outstanding features and impossible not to stare.

Had Garrett seen her as the car chugged past her down the hill? Probably not. Why would he look at pedestrians when he had someone beside him who... Words failed her. A tear slid down her cheek.

Rooted to the spot, she stared after the car that had long since disappeared. There seemed to be no reason to put one foot in front of the other. No reason to draw her next breath. Suspecting Garrett might be courting someone else had been bad enough. Actually *seeing him* with someone was so much worse, especially someone so beautiful.

Polly had never thought herself plain. The face she saw in the mirror each morning had its own charm, but she couldn't compete with the raven-haired beauty who had been clutching Garrett. There was something so *seductive* about her. Not a word Polly had ever used, but it seemed to suit the girl. No—woman. One had to describe her as a woman.

Polly's feet began to take her numb mind and body back to town. Why had Mother sent her here? She couldn't remember. Kitt waved again from across the street, then went on when Polly didn't respond.

As she reached the edge of town, Polly's heart shattered and broke. She ran as she hadn't run since she was a child, stumbling in her haste. There were hurts even a mother couldn't heal, but her feet took her in the direction of the only person to whom she'd always gone.

CHAPTER 16

Blinded by tears and bent almost double from the pain in her side, Polly stumbled up the porch steps and struggled to open the heavy front door. When it yielded, she almost fell into the warm living room. Not bothering to take off her boots or coat, she staggered straight to the kitchen where her mother prepared dinner.

Eyes wide, Mother started toward her, dropping her dish towel.

"Mother, oh Mother," Polly sobbed, throwing herself into her astonished mother's arms. "Mother, I can't bear it."

Without a word, her mother held her close and smoothed her hair as she had when she was a child. She rocked Polly gently and crooned, "There, there, it will be all right, dear. Hush now, Little One, please don't cry."

Elsie and Twila dropped their long-handled wooden spoons with a clatter, forgetting the pretend dinner they'd been stirring. Maggie and Beth's voices from the dining room stopped in mid-sentence as Polly's weeping continued. They appeared in the doorway.

"Mother, what's the matter with Polly? Why is she crying?"

"I don't know, Beth. Sometimes big people get hurt in ways that are hard for little people to understand. Florence will tell me when she's ready. Go on now, all of you. Maggie, take the children into the parlor and read them a story."

"Want Pa-we," Twila resisted, while Elsie mourned, "Pa-we cwy."

Beth patted Polly's cheek as she left the room. The kitchen grew quiet except for the faint sound of Elsie still repeating from the front room, "Pa-we cwy. Pa-we cwy."

Polly's sobs began to quiet although she still hiccupped and gasped for breath every few seconds. Finally, Mother led her to the dining room table, pushed her gently into a chair and seated herself beside her. "Are you ready to tell me about it?"

Taking off her scarf and mittens, Polly began to unbutton her coat, avoiding her mother's eyes. When would she outgrow this childish behavior? She'd cried on her mother's shoulder twice recently. This growing up business was much harder than Polly had expected.

At last, she raised her head and met her mother's kind, questioning eyes. "I'm sorry for being such a baby." Her words sounded jerky, her breath coming in ragged gasps.

Mother squeezed her hand, then pulled a clean, linen handkerchief from her pocket. Tenderly she wiped Polly's eyes and pressed the handkerchief into her clenched hand. "What happened, Little One?"

The term of endearment undid Polly and fat, hot tears slid down her cheeks again. "I saw Garrett drive into town with a beautiful woman in his car. I suspected he might be seeing someone else but I never thought it would be someone like *her*."

"What's so special about this woman?"

Polly wrinkled her forehead. "Her looks were—" Mother might not approve of the word *seductive*. "Spectacular, sensational, I guess. The kind of woman everyone stares at—especially men."

Mother nodded, her dark brown eyes comprehending. "That surprised you?"

"Devastated is more like it. I'm devastated that Garrett's seeing someone else. Devastated that she's so beautiful. I convinced myself he was in love with me, although he never said so, and that we would get married some day."

Mother squeezed her hand and said, "Florence, I'm not sorry Garrett has found someone else. You know how I've felt about him from the start."

She stroked Polly's cheek. "But I am sorry that you're hurting and feeling such pain. Losing something precious is always hard whether it's good for us or not. The Bible says God is near to the broken hearted and those that are crushed in spirit."

Polly pulled her hand from her mother's. She didn't want to hear about God right now. He had betrayed her just as He had betrayed Sarah Davis—the only difference being that Sarah hadn't realized it. Sarah had continued putting her faith in Him even though He had failed her many times. Polly didn't intend to make the same mistake. She moved her chair a few inches away from Mother.

"I know you want to help, but if God is near to the brokenhearted, why doesn't He do something to keep their hearts from being broken? If He's as powerful as you say, that shouldn't be hard for Him."

Mother wrinkled her brow. "Sometimes the reason He doesn't do something is because He won't interfere with our free will. He can see the path we're on will lead to heartbreak, but He allows it because of the choices we make."

Polly stood up. How could her mother be so blind? She was just like Sarah, always believing the best about God. What kind of a God didn't interfere if He knew the path we were on would lead to heartbreak?

"Then there are other times," Mother gazed out the window, "when trouble and pain come because we live in a fallen world with sin and sickness and disease. While God isn't the author of evil, He allows it."

She polished the table with her thumb. "He will use it, if we'll let Him, to produce qualities in us that would never be developed if our lives stayed sunny and pain free."

Polly walked to the window and looked out at the fading sun. She loved sunshine and blue skies as much as she hated pain. Weren't there other ways for God to shape her character? "Shouldn't creating happiness and removing pain be important to God, too?"

"I know those are two of your most important goals, Florence. Nevertheless, we can't create God in our own image. He's bigger than that."

Mother's eyes were filled with deep concern and sympathy when Polly turned from the window, but Polly didn't respond. How could she tell her mother she didn't think much of her God?

There was a gentle tug on Polly's skirt. She looked down into Twila's anxious blue eyes. "I'm all right." Stooping, she drew Twila close, smoothing her corn silk, fine blond hair. "Don't worry, Sweet Baby."

Twila smiled as Polly kissed her little sister's cheek. If she as a big sister was so willing to do everything in her power to make her sister happy and pain free, why wouldn't God do the same for her?

Avoiding her mother's eyes, Polly stood, kicked off her heavy boots and shrugged out of her bulky winter coat. She gathered Twila into her arms and walked out of the dining room.

CHAPTER 17

Polly lay on her bed, staring at the ceiling. Things were simpler when she was a child and could lose herself in a game of make-believe. But try as she might, she couldn't conjure up any exotic beasts from the patterns made by the lengthening shadows. The fading light only added to her feeling of gloom. Maybe she was so emotionally dead that her imagination was completely gone.

Closing her eyes, Polly pulled her sister's pillow over her face but couldn't blot out the memories. Each time the mental picture of Garrett seated beside his new love returned, the features of the woman became more and more Goddess-like.

With a little sob, Polly flung the pillow across the room, narrowly missing a glass of water Maggie had left on the bureau. She pushed herself to a sitting position. *If I turn against God, to whom will I go for the comfort and strength I need to get through the days ahead?* Those were the words Sarah had written in her diary after losing the daughter she loved.

What was the use of having a God who couldn't be trusted to keep bad things from happening?

A light knock sounded on her door. It was probably Mother, and Polly wasn't ready to talk to her again. "Go away," she called in a carefully controlled voice. "I don't want to talk to you."

"Florence, it's me." Her father's deep voice penetrated the closed door. "May I come in?"

Polly was so surprised that for a moment she was speechless. Father hadn't come to her room to talk since she was a little girl. He claimed her mother knew best when it came to raising young women, and he rarely got involved. "I—I guess so."

Her father's steps were tentative as he entered and stopped in front of her. He stared at the floor, opening and closing his hands.

What had Mother told him? He couldn't have missed her disheveled appearance even in the dimness of late afternoon.

A few moments ticked by as Father opened his mouth, then closed it again. What did he want? "Would you like to sit down?" She scooted over.

Nodding, he lowered himself to the edge of the bed with a heavy sigh. "Florence." He raked his thick hand through his hair. "I'm not very good with words at a time like this."

So Mother had told him about Garrett.

"But there are some things I need to say. I've never interfered with your dates with Garrett because the lessons we learn ourselves, even if it's through making mistakes, are the ones that benefit us most. I've bitten my tongue many times over the past few months to keep from telling you things I hoped you'd find out for yourself."

"What kind of things?"

"Things about Garrett. More than anything else, Florence, I want you to marry a man you can trust. A man who says the same things 'out of both sides of his mouth.' Garrett is not that kind of man. Time after time, I found out the stories he told you were nothing but lies. He's earned himself the reputation of a liar in our town."

Clasping his hands, Father sat up straighter. "All the while, he was leading you to believe he loved you, he was seeing at least two other girls."

Polly jumped up. "Why didn't you tell me?" She wrapped her blanket tighter around her and paced the cold floor. "How could you let me go on seeing him?"

"Because I didn't think you'd believe *me* until you saw it with your own eyes. You were so determined not to see his faults, I felt it best to let you find out for yourself."

Much as she hated to admit it, Polly suspected her father was right. There had been many times when she'd excused Garrett's behavior in spite of her mother's warnings. On the few occasions when she'd tried to talk to him about her concerns,

Garrett had always accused her of sounding like her mother instead of answering her questions.

"You think this is a terrible tragedy." Her father squinted at her. "Wouldn't it have been far worse to find out these things after you were married to Garrett? Someday you'll be thankful you learned the truth about him when you did."

Polly sighed and shook her head. "He might have changed."

"Maybe he would. People do sometimes, albeit after a lot of years of heartache and pain for the people who love them."

There was that word again—was there no way to escape it? "I hate pain." Polly plopped on the bed and stifled a sob. "I hate it, I hate it."

Her father's work-roughened hand massaged Polly's neck. Was he regretting his attempt to talk to his temperamental daughter? She sat up at last and tried to tidy her hair. "I'm sorry. I thought I was almost an adult. It looks like I have a long way to go."

"We all have a lot to learn no matter what our age."

"Even you?"

"Even me. Maybe if I'd spent more time with you, I could have taught you what important character traits to look for in a man. It was a mistake to think girls only need their mothers."

Father's words began to fill up some of her emptiness, emptiness she hadn't even realized existed. She had just accepted that, after a certain age, boys needed their fathers and girls needed their mothers, never realizing something was missing. Polly threw her arms around her father's neck in a way she hadn't done for a very long time. "I think you're right, Papa." The childhood name slipped out. "I *have* needed time with you, and I didn't even know what I lacked. I love you, Papa."

"I love you, too, Shorty."

Polly had almost forgotten her father's nickname for her.

"Now," holding her away from him, he lifted her chin. "I promised your mother I'd try to convince you to eat some supper. I'd hate to break my word. Do you think you're up to it?"

Straightening her shoulders and looking her father in the eye, Polly managed a smile. She didn't want him to know the knot in the pit of her stomach made it difficult to think about food. No sense in causing him any more worry. Putting her hand through the crook of his arm, Polly tried to sound cheerful. "I'm ready if you are."

CHAPTER 18

Sitting in the dimly lit church on the slatted wooden bench with the rest of her family, Polly listened to the organ playing Christmas carols. It was the first Sunday of Advent so she suspected today's sermon would reflect one of the standard pre-Christmas messages she'd heard since she was a little girl. Did ministers reach into dusty files marked "Advent" and pull out messages from days gone by? At least she could enjoy the music.

Polly smothered a sigh as the last chords of *O Come, O Come, Emmanuel* faded. Pastor Lawrence stood up. "This morning I have a pleasant surprise for you. Reverend James Caldwell from Ohio is visiting relatives and has agreed to bring our morning message. Pastor Caldwell, it's a pleasure to have you here."

The visiting pastor looked at least 20 years younger than their pastor. As he stood behind the rough wooden pulpit, Polly sat up straighter. Maybe they wouldn't be having leftovers after all. The young man shifted from one foot to the other as he opened his Bible and cleared his throat.

"Our text today is John 11:6." He coughed before he began to read. *When Jesus had heard, therefore, that Lazarus was sick, he abode two days still in the same place where he was.*

Reverend Caldwell's gaze roved over the small congregation. "You may think this is a strange text for the first Sunday of Advent. However, I believe the Holy Spirit is prompting me to preach this message."

The young pastor had Polly's attention. She'd never heard any minister say the Holy Spirit had interfered with what he wanted to preach. At Advent?

"I want you to look closely at this verse because it contradicts one of our misconceptions of how God should work in our lives.

"John begins this unusual chapter by telling us, 'Jesus loved Martha, and her sister, and Lazarus.' Yet when notified of Lazarus' illness, he didn't rush to alleviate their pain." He paused. "Instead, He stayed where He was for two days."

Polly squirmed in her seat.

Reverend Caldwell continued, "How do you think Martha felt about Jesus' tardiness?"

Was he looking straight at her?

"Do we dare believe it is not *in spite of* God's unchanging love for us but *because of it* that He doesn't always immediately relieve our pain? Do we dare believe that sometimes suffering is God's good gift to produce qualities we wouldn't develop any other way?"

Polly's resistance to his words was crumbling. The hard knot in her stomach that had made eating difficult loosened a little. She looked at her mother just as she turned her head in Polly's direction. Her dark brown eyes shone with tears.

The minister's intense gaze swept the congregation. "Even though pain was not part of God's original plan for His perfect world, I believe it's part of His plan for bringing restoration to His fallen world. Many have found that enduring sorrow and suffering as traveling companions on their life journey has led them to greater spiritual heights than good fortune and gladness could ever have produced."

There was an uncharacteristic hush over the little congregation. Reverend Caldwell leaned toward them, his earnestness and desire to communicate God's truth apparent. "However, only those who remain pliable in the Potter's hands will find this to be true. The choice is always ours. Will we allow ourselves to be molded, shaped and changed into the image of Christ by our pain or will we become brittle, hard and easily shattered by the tragedies we encounter?"

It was obvious what choice Sarah Davis had made. She had swayed and wobbled under the blows—blows much more severe than the one Polly was weathering, but her faith had never wavered. What was the secret of Sarah's strength, her ability to make the right choice? Polly wished she knew.

Unbidden, the words of this morning's hymn replayed in her mind, "O Come, O Come, Emmanuel." Emmanuel. *God with us.* What had Sarah learned about Emmanuel, God with us, that Polly hadn't?

♠

Closing Sarah's diary and dropping it into her lap, Polly shook her head in disbelief. Reading the contents of this journal had again left her in awe of the woman who had penned the words with such strength and courage. Polly could hardly comprehend the series of hills and valleys she'd read about today. What would it have been like actually to *experience* the highs and lows of that four-year period?

Thomas and Sarah had suffered the loss of their eldest daughter, Mary, in 1867. Less than a year later, their second born, Elizabeth, had gotten married. In 1869, they celebrated the birth of their first grandchild, Naomi, only to be faced with the death of their twenty-year-old daughter, Sarah Lucinda, the following year. Six months later, they rejoiced in the birth of their second grandchild, Harry. Five months after that, they experienced the loss of their daughter, Elizabeth, the mother of these two babies.

Grateful for the joys but grieving the sorrows, Sarah had poured out her pain. While clinging to God, her source of strength, she clutched tightly the children still in her care. Although she hadn't been able to protect the precious offspring she'd lost, she made renewed efforts to shield the ones that remained.

Those efforts had not deterred her oldest son, Robert, from going west after the loss of his three sisters. With the completion of the transcontinental railroad, nothing stood between him and the dreams he'd fostered ever since gold had been discovered in Colorado eleven years earlier. At the age of twenty-five, he was old enough to do as he pleased, but Sarah prayed continually for his return.

Polly wished she'd had the opportunity to meet this woman. In the beginning, her interest had been in discovering the reason behind the chilling sensations she experienced in this house; now it seemed Sarah'd had something more important to teach her than Polly had at first believed.

Why did my faith crumble into bitterness and anger at the first sign of troubled waters while Sarah's faith survived stormy winds and crashing waves that would have sunk many ships?

Sliding the diary back under her pillow, Polly sprawled across the bed—a rare luxury since her share was usually one third—and closed her eyes. The image of Garrett and his raven-haired beauty still gripped her more often than she wanted. On occasions like today when the pain became devastating, she focused on the things her father had told her about Garrett. The reminder that her perception of him had been an illusion helped ease the pain.

Even so, remembering his kisses and tender words created an intense yearning. Would she be able to refuse him should he ever come back to her? How could she even consider it now that she knew the truth? Her mind and body were at war in a never-ending battle—her mind logically stating the facts while her body and her emotions cried for reciprocated love. Would she ever find peace?

CHAPTER 19

Polly traced patterns in the leaded glass window with the tip of her finger as huge, fluffy snowflakes drifted down from the leaden sky. *I should probably do something about decorating the house for Christmas, but I'm not in the mood.* Mother hadn't been feeling well for several weeks and wasn't up to taking on added responsibilities. This time Dr. Cooley had confirmed this wasn't a false alarm—Mother was pregnant.

Amazing what a difference seven months could make. Last spring, Polly had been upset that Mother might be pregnant because it would mean less time with Garrett. Now with him out of the picture, she was concerned at the toll another pregnancy might take on her mother's health. She'd heard the risk of complications increased with age even though it wasn't unusual for women to give birth at forty.

Trying to shake off her gloom, Polly went back to the problem at hand. If any decorating was to be done, she would have to do it.

"How about joining me on the hill to gather some ground pine to decorate the house, Shorty?" She started at her father's voice. "Now might be a good time while Mother and the little ones are napping."

Much as she appreciated her father's efforts, even calling her by her nickname, she couldn't shake the lethargy that weighed her down. But she didn't want to disappoint him as he watched her with a hopeful smile. "All right, Papa, just let me get my coat."

In a few minutes, Polly and her father set out, bundled up enough to have pleased even Mother in all their winter trappings.

Only their eyes and noses were exposed. The wind whipped around them as they walked to the overgrown bank behind the house where the slope wasn't as steep. There were other places they could have found ground pine, but scaling hills was always something of an adventure—one that Polly and her father had enjoyed when she was a little girl. When Polly began to lag behind, her father reached out and took her hand just as he had years ago in Jackson Center.

As the silence lengthened, Father cleared his throat. "How are you doing, Florence?"

Polly knew his question had nothing to do with climbing the hill. She hesitated. It felt so strange to be talking to her father about anything other than the weather and household chores. At last she spoke, her voice slightly muffled by the scarf she'd tied around her face. "I'm not sure, Papa. I'm so mixed up. How can I have such strong feelings for someone even when I know he's not the person I thought he was?"

Papa's brown eyes were serious, his dark lashes flecked with snow. "That's a tough question. I guess it's because feelings aren't controlled by facts. We can't always change how we feel; yet we can choose not to act on our feelings."

Polly raised her eyebrows at her father's lengthy speech. His eyes twinkled. "At least, that's what your mother tells me."

They burst out laughing. She should have suspected he was just parroting Mother. They all looked to her for answers about things that puzzled them—whether about human nature, God or relationships. While Mother sometimes lacked physical strength, especially during and after pregnancies, she had strength in wisdom and knowledge, a trait they all relied on when life became difficult, even Father.

Their laughter dissolved the somber shroud that clung to them, and they began to talk of less serious things as they reached the top of the hill. Polly loved to brush away the thick white frosting to expose the lush ground pine that was plentiful under the snow. Father had brought a strong clipper to cut the thick vines and a gunnysack for carrying them. All too soon, the bag was overflowing. Even though her toes had grown numb from the cold, Polly didn't want to go back inside.

"You go ahead, Father. I think I'll stay up here for a while. It's too beautiful to go in yet."

Her father frowned. "Are you sure? The hill is tricky with all this snow. Shouldn't you come down with me?"

Polly hesitated. "I appreciate your concern, but I'm not ready to go in yet. I'll be okay." She patted her father's arm. "I'm a big girl now you know."

He squeezed Polly's hand, and then, shouldering his bag, he started down the hill. "Be careful," he called as she turned in the opposite direction.

Being up on this hill seemed to put things in perspective. Even though the thick falling snow hid most of the town, the height gave her a feeling of being above her circumstances. She also felt protected and secure with the curtain of snow shutting out the rest of the world. Maybe up here she could get some insight into what she had been experiencing lately.

The more despondent and discouraged Polly had become, the more she seemed to attract the negative vibrations in the house. She still had no clear-cut answer about the cause of them. There weren't many pages left in the worn, slender volume she'd hoped would answer her questions. Polly had been tempted to skim the pages looking for answers, but Mother had always discouraged them from sneaking peaks at the back of the book.

It might help to talk to Mother about her uneasy feelings about the house. Still, they seemed so subjective. How could she impose them on Mother when she wasn't feeling her best?

With a sigh, Polly turned around and started toward home. She wasn't getting any closer to resolving her misgivings. Recklessness gripped her. Rather than returning the way she and her father had come, she started down a more direct route at the steepest juncture of the hill. At first, the path wasn't too treacherous as she picked her way along, step-by-step, trying not to be deceived by the depth of the snow.

Then her left foot sank into a hole and became entangled with tree roots hidden by the thick white blanket. Polly fell facedown, feeling her left ankle twist beneath her. "Papa," she cried, lifting her head. "Papa, help! Please help!"

Polly's voice was muffled by her scarf, and the wind seemed to pick up her words and blow them back against the hill.

Stinging pains shot through her ankle and hot tears she'd held back for days melted the snow as they trickled down her cheeks. "Mother, oh Mother, what shall I do?"

At last, she managed to push herself onto her knees, her foot still stubbornly refusing to budge. Every wiggle she made in her attempts to dislodge it brought fresh tears. She yanked off her left mitten and reached behind her, scrapping away snow with her bare hand. Ignoring the pain, she grasped her ankle and gave a mighty tug. She shrieked as her foot came free, her boot flying through the air, and fell flat on her face again.

Not even bothering to raise her head, Polly sobbed into the snow.

Get up. You have to find your boot before it's covered with snow.

I can't. My ankle is killing me.

You have to...

Polly groaned as her inner dialogue continued. On hands and knees, she crawled in the direction her boot had flown, trying to keep her left foot off the ground. There it was. It had landed right side up so the inside was somewhat dry. Pushing herself up and balancing on one foot like a stork, she directed her foot into her boot. When she lowered her left foot and put a little weight on it, she staggered to one knee, pinpricks of light blurring her vision. In spite of the excruciating pain, she couldn't sit down and wait for help. She had very little feeling in her feet and her hands were numb. She had to keep moving.

Polly shuffled a few paces, wobbling with every step, before she lost her balance and fell again. Each time she fell, it became more and more difficult to force herself to her feet. Her ankle throbbed and her head ached. Each fall accentuated her pain. How bad could it be to lie back and rest for a few minutes?

As Polly shifted to a more comfortable position, she noticed a sturdy stick just out of reach almost covered with snow. That stick could help her walk if she could reach it. Her eyes closed. If only she weren't so tired.

One last spark of determination flared and she dragged herself to the stick, pushed to her knees, and grasped hold of it. Supporting herself with her newfound treasure, she stood up and continued the long, painstaking journey to the house that an hour ago had seemed so distasteful.

CHAPTER 20

The fire Father had built earlier snapped and crackled in the wood stove in the corner of the front room. Polly snuggled deeper into the blankets wrapped around her. She had occupied this spot on the davenport for most of the past few weeks. Funny how much colder the house seemed when one couldn't move about. Dr. Cooley said her ankle needed complete rest for at least two weeks. It wasn't broken but badly sprained.

In spite of her fall and Mother's early pregnancy fatigue, it had been one of the best Christmases ever. After the commotion of her accident died down, her father insisted the greenery must be hung. All the children got involved as Mother and Polly supervised. Even Twila and Elsie took bits of evergreen to put wherever they wanted. Everyone became a little giddy as Mother thanked God repeatedly that Polly had not gotten frostbite, caught pneumonia, or broken her ankle.

Mother had managed to get some little gifts ready for the children before she started feeling poorly. No one complained that the gifts were few. Instead, there was a sense of joy in being together as the snow continued to fall.

The love Polly's family showered on her as she lay enthroned in the front room had made Christmas special. Used to being the giver but so seldom the receiver, she hardly knew how to respond. Each gesture of love brought a little more thawing to the hard lump deep inside. Maybe her family *did* love her for herself, not just for the things she did.

It wouldn't be so hard for Polly to lie here if Mother had been feeling better. Even though Maggie and the boys tackled chores they'd never attempted, Mother still needed to supervise. Guilt engulfed her when she saw Mother's face, white and drawn by the end of the day. Still her mother insisted she obey the doctor's orders.

Maybe today Mother would allow her to get up or even climb the stairs. She wiggled her toes and turned her foot from side to side. *It feels stronger.* Polly itched to read the last pages of Sarah's diary. Out of reach up in her bedroom, it drew her.

I'd have to share my secret if I asked someone to bring it to me.

With sudden inspiration, Polly pushed the blankets aside and swung her legs over the edge of the couch. No one was up except Father and Ben who had gotten up early to break a path to work. School hadn't begun after Christmas vacation because of the continuing snowfall and bitter cold. No early morning stirring broke the stillness, and Polly had a plan.

Putting most of her weight on her right foot, she slowly stood up. The dull ache in her ankle was almost gone. After several steps, she convinced herself she could venture upstairs. Her two weeks were up today.

Polly's thick stockings not only protected her feet from the cold wooden steps but also muffled her footsteps. She crossed the landing and started up the stairs. Grateful to be on her feet, she was tempted to run. Two weeks of being an invalid was more than enough.

One of the floorboards creaked and she hesitated, listening for sounds from her mother's bedroom. Silence. Good thing Ben had gone with Father since his bedroom was closest to the stairs. Not that he was likely to wake up. Mother said Ben slept so sound he might be left behind when the last trump blew.

With a sigh of relief, Polly reached the top of the stairs and crept into the room where Maggie and Beth were sleeping. This would be the tricky part. She edged up close to the bed and slid her hand noiselessly under the pillow she and Beth shared. Getting a good grip on the diary without disturbing her sleeping sister wouldn't be easy.

Sometimes the slightest movement would cause Beth to sit upright while at other times waking her was impossible. At last Polly gave a gentle tug. The book moved several inches but so did

Beth. She turned her head so that her nose was just inches from Polly's arm, her breathing still slow and steady.

After a pause, Polly risked another slight tug, then another. At last she held the coveted prize in her hand. Suppressing a cheer, she clutched the diary to her pounding heart and started for the door. A sudden movement from Maggie prompted Polly to dart into the hall, her ankle twinging at the unaccustomed activity. She breathed a sigh of relief when no accusing voice called out.

Polly crept down the stairs and back under her blankets with no evidence she had ever left that cozy spot, aside from an occasional pang in her ankle. Now if only Mother and the rest of the family would sleep until she finished reading. She turned up the kerosene lamp Father had lit for her, and opened the book that had inspired admiration, fear, anger, confusion and so many other emotions during the past months.

January, 1875. I finally decided how to spend a portion of the inheritance from my dear parents' estate. We purchased land in Sandy Lake so that we can have a larger house built there.

Polly sat up straight. This was the first mention of the purchase of land to build a house in Sandy Lake. She turned a page.

I wish I were able to take more joy in this decision, but the reason for its necessity is still too painful for me to feel much emotion. After the loss of our precious Elizabeth, her husband, Samuel, wasn't able to care for their two children, as well as earn a living. He asked if we would raise little Harry and Naomi as our own.

I couldn't bring myself to agree without asking him to sign papers stating he wouldn't take the children from us later if he decided to remarry. Difficult as it is to think of raising two small children at our age, I couldn't bear the thought of treating them as our own, and then having them torn from me. Much as he loves his children, Edward agreed to my terms. He's so grief-stricken he believes he will never marry again. However, he's young and healthy and eventually perhaps his needs will overcome his grief.

So far, we've made do with the space we have, but I don't want Nancy, William, and Vance to feel crowded. Also, it's important to have room for Robert should he decide to come home. My children are of an age where many young people are thinking of marriage and finding a place of their own. Even so, I'm in no hurry for them to do that, especially when I have the funds for a larger house. I've always liked Sandy Lake, and Thomas will have no trouble starting a business there. He says he may decide to sell ready-made clothes and shoes for men and women.

The next entry, dated July 1876, went into detail about where each child would sleep. Excitement tingled in Polly's cheeks when she realized Sarah and Thomas had slept in the very room she currently shared with her sisters. She also noted with a little shiver that Vance had claimed the back bedroom where the oppression seemed strongest.

Many of the wall coverings Sarah described had not been changed. Delicately flowered lavender wallpaper graced Thomas and Sarah's bedroom, which seemed to fit the gentle spirit Polly often sensed as she read Sarah's diary.

The elegant red and gray paper that covered the walls of the front room where she now lay had once been Sarah's pride and joy. Her feeling of kinship with this extraordinary woman grew.

October, 1876. Moving day. Although I'm almost too weary to pick up my pen, I cannot let this day pass without noting it. We're all happily settled, or at least as settled as is possible with more unpacking to do. The essentials are in place. I pray God will grant Thomas and me long life here for the raising of our precious grandchildren. And for the sake of our older children who rely on us a great deal. My instincts to protect them are strong, and I worry that I've fostered a tendency to depend on me too much. Is it too late to change?

Footsteps on the stairs alerted Polly to tuck Sarah's diary out of sight before her mother entered the room. She had read more than half the book. Now that Sarah and her family had moved into this house, would the remaining pages answer her questions about the origin of the oppression?

CHAPTER 21

Knock, knock. Polly startled and moved to get up from the couch.

"Maggie, please answer the door." Mother's voice wafted in from the kitchen.

"I can get it." Polly raised her voice.

"No, you just rest."

Mother still insisted she keep her foot elevated as much as possible even though more than two weeks had passed.

Maggie ambled into the living room, book in hand. When she opened the door, Kitt Potter stood outside.

"Kitt, hello." Polly swung her legs down and pushed herself into a sitting position. "Please come in."

Maggie stepped aside and Kitt closed the door with a shy smile.

"I heard yesterday you'd sprained your ankle."

"I'm better now. Except Mother still insists I take it easy." Kitt's eyes roamed the room. Did she compare their humble living quarters with her more expensive house? Kitt's rich heritage made Polly uncomfortable at times.

"Can we go into the sitting room to talk?" Kitt spoke in a low voice, twisting the fingers of her winter gloves.

Polly glanced at Maggie who had stopped reading to listen. "Sure."

Kitt reached for Polly's arm as she stood up. "I'm fine. Really."

They went into the sitting room, and Kitt closed the door behind them. Polly sank down on the faded velveteen loveseat and motioned for Kitt to do the same. She waited for Kitt to begin but she remained silent. "So how was your Christmas holiday?"

Kitt shrugged. "It was okay. Nothing has been the same since Papa, George, and Charles are gone."

Polly knew Kitt's family had lost her father and two brothers over eight years time. Her father had died when Kitt was fifteen. "I can't imagine how painful that would be, losing three people so dear to you."

Kitt nodded and gave a wistful smile. She smoothed her hand over the arm of the loveseat. "Mother tries her best but with just her, Bess, and me, that big house is so lonely."

"That must be hard."

The silence grew long. Polly stared at the door. Why had Kitt felt it necessary to close the door?

Kitt cleared her throat, sat up a little taller and gave half a nod. "Polly, do you know anything about Physical Culture?"

"Well, some..." Polly shrugged. "I've heard it has to do with health and physical fitness, and I've seen classes advertised. Why?"

"I am *very* interested in Physical Culture. I've been interested ever since I saw 'The Perfect Woman' at the Walter Main Circus in Sharon before Papa died. The advertisements said her faultless appearance of form and development was entirely due to the practice of Physical Culture."

Did Kitt memorize this stuff? "I know the ads said that but..." Polly doubted exercising and taking care of one's body could be *that* effective. And what was so secretive about Physical Culture? "Are you thinking of taking a class?"

"I've already taken some classes." Kitt looked down at her flat chest. "They don't seem to be helping much though."

Polly touched Kitt 's arm. "Most girls would be happy to have such a tiny waist."

"I'm past 20 years old, and I still look like a boy. There must be something wrong with me."

"Have you thought about seeing Dr. Cooley?"

"No, Mother thinks I'm being silly and I shouldn't bother my brother-in-law with such foolishness. Anyway, I'd be embarrassed."

Polly bit her lip. She didn't know what to say. If Polly had complained about her own figure, her mother would have told her to be thankful she was healthy and had enough to eat. Then again, maybe people who had plenty of money had higher expectations for their lives than those who had fewer resources.

"What are you going to do?"

"I don't know." Kitt smoothed her skirt. "I've been writing to... Oh, never mind."

Polly leaned forward and stared at Kitt. "Who have you been writing to?"

"Just forget it. I shouldn't have said anything. He said not to."

"Kitt..."

"No, let's talk about something else. How did you hurt your ankle?"

Still frowning, Polly told her what had happened. "Good as new now. I wish Mother would stop being over protective."

"Have you seen Garrett lately?"

Polly's stomach lurched as it always did when she heard Garrett's name. "Not lately. Have you?"

"Well..." Kitt turned away, not meeting Polly's eyes.

"It's okay. I know he's seeing someone else."

"Yes, he fell hard, from what I hear. She lives in Jackson Center."

Polly cringed. "Do you know her?"

"No, town gossip says she's from Georgia. That's all I know." Kitt got up and started for the door. "I shouldn't have bothered you with my problems when you have problems of your own."

Grabbing her hand, Polly stood up. "It's okay. I'm worried about you. Are you sure you can't tell me who you're writing to? Why didn't he want you to tell me?"

"Not you personally, Polly. He doesn't want me to tell anyone."

"But Kitt..."

"I wanted advice, but I can't expect you to tell me what to do."

Polly bit her lip and clung to Kitt's hand, then let go. What could she do? Kitt was an adult. "All right then." She opened the sitting room door. "Thanks for stopping by. Visit anytime."

"Thanks, Polly." Kitt sighed. "I envy you your big happy family."

Polly's eyebrows rose as the laughter and teasing of her brothers and sisters swirled around them. Kitt envied *her?* Then again, all the money in the world couldn't take the place of the father or two brothers Kitt had lost.

She hugged Kitt's slight shoulders. It wasn't enough. There had to be something more she could do, some way to help her friend.

CHAPTER 22

The bell chimed as a distinguished man in a gray fedora hat entered the clothing store where Garrett worked. Yet another face without a name in his new environment. He missed seeing his friends and neighbors in Sandy Lake. However, visiting Savannah on his way home almost every day more than made up for that slight disadvantage.

"Good morning, sir." Garrett smiled.

The broad-shouldered man reached the counter, his expression stern. "Are you Garrett Young?"

Garrett's eyebrows rose. "Why, yes. May I help you?"

The man shook his head. "I'm from Jackson Center. I've seen you with Savannah Stevens."

"Really?" Garrett's forehead creased in a frown. Who *was* this fellow?

"Son, I think there are a few things about Savannah you should know."

Garrett's frown deepened. Why was this man involving himself in his affairs? "I don't know what you mean." He backed away a few steps.

"I'm Maxwell Sullivan, and if you're smart, you'll listen to what I have to say."

He stared at the man. "Why should I listen to you? I don't even know you."

Mr. Sullivan took off his hat. His expression softened. "I have a son about your age, and if he were doing what you are, I'd want someone to tell him what I'm about to tell you."

"I'm not doing anything wrong." *I've never known anyone like Savannah, and I want to marry her.* It was the first time Garrett had even thought those words. To his surprise, he discovered he meant them. Never before had someone stolen his heart.

Mr. Sullivan leaned on the counter and lowered his voice. "Do you know what Savannah does for a living?"

Garrett shrugged. "We've never discussed it. I assumed her parents send her money from Georgia."

"That's what I thought." He put his hand on Garrett's shoulder, but Garrett brushed it off and glared at him.

"What does it matter how she earns a living? Do you think I'd care if she washed dishes or scrubbed floors?"

"Savannah doesn't wash dishes or scrub floors, Mr. Young. She entertains gentlemen in her room above the tavern. It's become quite a lucrative business."

"No. I don't believe you." Garrett started toward the broad-shouldered customer, his hands clenching into fists.

"Keep your voice down. Do you want your boss to hear you?"

"Savannah would never do such a thing." Did he really believe that? If Savannah had allowed him to take certain liberties in the short time he'd known her, she might be capable of what Mr. Sullivan claimed.

"The sheriff has chosen to look the other way, although it's only a matter of time. Eventually enough concerned citizens will raise a fuss that he'll have to put a stop to it."

Mr. Black, Garrett's boss, came out of the office, and Mr. Sullivan turned toward the door. With one last look at Mr. Black, he turned back to Garrett. "How do you think Savannah got you this job?" He walked out of the store.

Bile burned in Garrett's throat. He brushed a hand over his eyes. Mr. Sullivan had to be mistaken. The new world he'd been building the past few weeks was trembling around him. Could his job have been payment for favors as that loathsome man implied? A lot of people didn't think much of *his* morals but this—*this* was unbelievable.

Garrett stared at the polished hardwood floor shaking his head. Mr. Black's voice startled him. "What's wrong? Was there a problem with Mr. Sullivan?"

"No, no problem with Mr. Sullivan, but I'm not feeling well. I must be getting sick."

"Perhaps you should take the rest of the day off. Mondays are often slow. If you're sick, we can't have you infecting the customers."

Before Mr. Black had finished speaking, Garrett headed for the back door. He stopped to pick up his coat and hat. Maybe he could find Savannah and get this misunderstanding cleared up.

"See you tomorrow if you're feeling up to it."

With a half nod, Garrett stepped outside, pulling the door closed behind him. Shutting his eyes, he leaned against it, his legs trembling and nausea coming in waves. Maybe he *was* getting sick—no, he was just sick over Mr. Sullivan's accusations.

Why would the man take it upon himself to find Garrett? He'd said he had a son about Garrett's age. Maybe his son and Savannah had been courting. Maybe Mr. Sullivan wanted Garrett to break things off so his son and Savannah could get back together. *Yes, that must be it. It's not going to work.*

He started the car and headed toward Jackson Center. How could he ask Savannah about Mr. Sullivan's accusations without making her angry? Maybe he could ask other people in the town rather than asking Savannah. No, he couldn't risk ruining her reputation. He would have to talk to her.

♠

Savannah blinked at Garrett when he found her having lunch in the dining room at the inn. "Garrett. What are you doing here? Shouldn't you be at work? Or did you plan to surprise me by having lunch with me?"

She purred the last words as she batted her long eyelashes and reached to touch his hand. In the past, her words and actions would have caused shivers of delight. Now they turned his stomach. Mr. Sullivan's accusations rang through his mind. *It's quite a lucrative business.* Garrett hated the man for making him question whether Savannah's behavior was part of a much-practiced act.

Much like your own behavior in the past with whomever you happened to be courting that day. Where did that thought come from? That was all in the past. Now that he'd fallen in love with Savannah, there'd be no more of that.

"What's wrong?" Savannah peered at him.

Garrett looked away and rubbed his chin.

She stretched her hand toward him. "Since you're here, why don't you sit down and have a cup of tea?"

"Okay." Garrett started to sit, then changed his mind. "On second thought, if you're almost finished, would you come for a ride? I need to talk to you, and I'd rather not do it here."

Savannah's brows shot up. She put down her fork. "What do you want to talk about?"

"Not here. Will you come?"

She stared into her teacup, then nodded. "All right, just give me a few minutes to finish my lunch."

"I don't feel well. I think I'll step outside to get some air."

"I'll be out in a minute."

Garrett nodded, then headed for the door.

Time dragged as he waited for Savannah to join him. The air was so cold he could see his breath. *What in the world am I going to say to her?*

At last, the front door opened and Savannah stepped outside, looking glamorous in her stylish fur coat. How could she afford a coat like that? Garrett moved to open the car door for her, but then turned back and let Savannah get in by herself. He'd been treating her like a first-class lady.

His Model T started with a roar as he twisted the crank. Soon they were motoring down the road. Garrett had never enjoyed it less.

Savannah looked at him, a puzzled frown marring her forehead. "What did you want to talk to me about?"

Gripping the steering wheel, Garrett stared straight ahead. "Do you know Mr. Sullivan?"

She shrugged one shoulder. "He has a store in Jackson Center."

"Did you date his son?"

"We've never dated. I think I know who he is. Why do you ask?"

Garrett shook his head, trying to hide his disappointment. "Mr. Sullivan came to see me at the store today."

Savannah played with the clasp of her beaded burgundy handbag. "Did he need a new coat?"

Garrett kept his eyes on the road. "He came to warn me about you."

The clasp of Savannah's purse stopped snapping. "Oh."

He waited for her to defend herself or to ask why Mr. Sullivan had warned him. She said nothing. Garrett gritted his teeth as the silence became unbearable.

"I was hoping you would never need to know."

He swerved and with a squeal of brakes, stopped the car. "So it's true." The whole car seemed to vibrate with his roar as he turned off the engine.

"It's true."

"But why? Why would you choose that lifestyle? And why would you lead me to think you were a decent, God-fearing woman?"

"I never said I was a decent, God-fearing woman. I've chosen this life-style because I like the things money can buy, same as you. I don't have wealthy parents to buy them for me like you do."

Garrett gripped the steering wheel. "But why did you encourage me to believe you were interested in me?"

"I am interested in you. I thought if you didn't know the truth, you might ask me to marry you—then I could have the things I want, as well as a respectable life. I'd prefer that to the life I'm living."

"So you don't really love me? You just want me for what you can get from me?"

"I like you very much. We both want the same things out of life, so perhaps we'd be very happy together."

With an angry snort, Garrett got out to crank the car to life, then settled back behind the wheel. "I can't believe you'd do this to me, Savannah. How many other men are you deceiving?"

"I think you'd better take me home." Savannah flounced on her seat. "I knew you'd be angry if you found out the truth. Still, I'd hoped you would see things my way and agree we're well suited for each other." She wrapped her fingers around the door handle. "Maybe after you've had time to think it over, you'll change your mind."

"You were just using me."

Savannah looked at him with those penetrating, deep violet eyes. "Is this the first time you've been on the receiving end?"

Garrett felt his neck and checks get hot as Savannah's gaze bored deeper. "How does it feel, Garrett? How does it feel?"

CHAPTER 23

Polly snuggled under the blanket and pulled her chair closer to the woodstove. Spring still seemed far away. Earlier this week, she'd helped Blanche and George with their valentines for school. She wished they could have fancy ones like Kit Potter always had when they were in school but she'd done her best.

She missed those days of exchanging valentines, but most people her age only gave valentines to their sweethearts. She sat up straighter. *I will not think about Garrett.*

Mother and the little ones were resting, so Polly settled in to read more of Sarah's diary. Why was she hesitant to read the remaining pages? Perhaps she feared the diary had no answers for her. Polly sighed and opened the journal.

May 18, 1878. Thomas gathered ripe strawberries from our garden this morning for the first time. Our unseasonably warm winter probably accounts for the early berries. Last year we got very few—that's to be expected the first year of planting.

Polly's mouth watered. She loved strawberries.

A month from today, Thomas plans to take a trip to the Old Country. He'll be gone three or four months, visiting Ireland, England, Scotland, and a Paris exposition. He's been longing for "home" where he was born. I'm not a good traveler, so I turned down his invitation to go. The house will be quiet without the warmth of his presence. Vance will finish the last preparations on the store they'll open when Thomas returns.

If only Polly could have known Thomas and Sarah. How could a house they'd owned have such a sense of darkness at times?

October 1878. We've been enjoying our new home and getting to know some of the people in Sandy Lake. Thomas's trip went well and he and Vance opened a clothing and shoe store when Thomas returned. It's a new kind of business but they seem to enjoy it. Thomas has made many friends though my transplanting into the community has been slower. Sometimes we go back to visit friends in Sheakleyville.

Which store had the Davis's owned? Polly would have to ask someone. Thirty years wasn't such a long time ago.

July 5, 1879. Today we received news I've both dreaded and feared since William left three months ago to work for the railroad in Ohio, Indiana, and Illinois. The telegram read, "Met with accident. Arm amputated. Come. W. T. Davis." Vance left immediately to bring his brother home from Illinois since Thomas is troubled by rheumatism.

One good thing will come from this. Will's days of working on the railroad are over. He never liked being so far from home, just went because the pay was good. I pray I'll be able to support him as he recovers.

Another tragedy for Sarah, but at least Will hadn't lost his life. Polly put a log on the fire. Did Sarah curl up beside this stove to write in her journal? Probably not in July.

July 11, 1879. Will and Vance travelled home by train as soon as Will was able. His arm was run over by a train of cars in Illinois and cut off above the elbow. He's doing as well as can be expected in this heat. I'm so happy to have him home.

February 4, 1880. Thomas still struggles with inflammatory rheumatism and has been confined to his bed. I wish I knew a cure for this ailment. Vance runs the store but still seeks advice from his father. Thomas' cheerful presence is so missed at the store. I try not to worry about the occasional pains in my chest. Someone has to keep the family going.

Pains in Sarah's chest. That didn't sound good.

November 11, 1880. (Harry's tenth birthday). One thing I've learned, it's not as easy to raise one's grandchildren as it is to raise one's children. Now that Naomi is 11 and Harry is 10, life is simpler. Still I tire easily and my blood pressure has been high.

Polly rubbed her eyes and allowed herself to skim Sarah's spidery handwriting, shakier than before. Silver had been discovered in Leadville, Colorado, so the chances were slim R. J. would come home to stay. A huge disappointment for Sarah.

Will had physically recovered from the loss of his arm, although he still struggled emotionally. He worked in the orchard he and Thomas had planted on top of the hill behind their house—Thomas's compromise between moving to town while still maintaining their country life.

I'd say our move to Sandy Lake has been a success, although it was a bit of a wrench to leave behind our five dear girls in the Sheakleyville Cemetery. But I know it's only their bodies we left. Their spirits are safe in the arms of Jesus.

Polly let out her breath in a sigh of relief. It had been almost ten years since Naomi and Harry's mother had died, and apparently there had been no deaths since then. Although Polly's questions about the house remained unanswered, at least Sarah hadn't experienced any more severe losses.

Sarah hadn't mentioned chest pains in her last entry. Polly turned a page.

October 1885. Five years have passed since I've written in this little book. I've hidden my diary because these are private thoughts, but after I'm gone, I suppose it would do no harm for someone to read it. (Polly hugged herself and smiled at what seemed like Sarah's permission for her to read her journal.)

I've never told anyone about the loose board in Vance's bedroom. It seemed like a fine place to hide my journal. If I'd told Thomas, he would have been upset by the carpenter's carelessness, so I've kept it to myself. If Vance ever notices the squeaky board, he never mentions it.

Three days ago, I had a real scare. I had such a sharp pain in my chest that I cried out for help.

Polly wasn't skimming now but reading every word.

Everyone was gone except Nancy and me, so I asked her to go for the Doctor. Instead, she cowered in a corner and buried her head in her arms. I don't know what would've happened if Thomas hadn't come to get some paperwork. He ran for the doctor who happened to be in his office. Doc Cooley came and told me to rest in bed until we know what's wrong. I'm so thankful this didn't happen when Naomi and Harry were younger.

I'm more concerned about Nancy than I am about myself. Even as a child she had periods of darkness—some worse than others. She'll be forty in two years, and this time is the worst. She feels so guilty for failing me. Nothing I say makes her believe I've forgiven her. She sits and stares out the window and seems lost in her own dark world. Thomas says he had an aunt who behaved this way in Ireland.

Polly raised her head. Did the darkness Polly sensed in this house have something to do with the darkness Nancy had experienced? Poor Nancy.

Thomas still has his store, though he struggles with rheumatism from time to time. He and Vance work together to keep things going there while William works in the orchard. We've hired a woman to come and help with the cooking and cleaning until I'm able to be up again.

Not many entries left. She'd read one more and then try to get a few chores done before the children woke up.

June 1890. Another five years have gone by. How time flies. A few weeks after my last entry, Dr. Cooley said my heart wasn't strong and I must be careful. We had to keep our hired girl because Nancy can't be counted on. She struggles so.

Was Nancy feeble-minded? What would become of her when Sarah died?

Naomi married a fine young man last year and they're doing well. I just worry about his itching to go west. Harry is interested in a girl from Pittsburgh who has family in Sandy Lake. Wouldn't be surprised if they marry soon.

Seems strange that my grandchildren are marrying while my children aren't. Maybe I didn't hold on to them as tight because I'd learned to trust the Lord better by the time we raised them. Sometimes I worry that I've damaged our children. Yet I have to admit I'm happy to have all of them but Robert (for whom I continually pray) close to me, after having lost so many dear ones. I pray the Lord will allow me to live to see my great grandchildren.

"Pa-we, Pa-we." Twila and Elsie's voices blended into one from the nursery. Polly slipped the diary into her pocket although she longed to read more. For months, this little book had been her own delicious secret. It added an element of mystery and excitement to her life. After she finished reading it, what would she have to look forward to?

CHAPTER 24

Polly wandered across the living room to where Twila and Elsie were playing with dolls. She watched them for a few moments, then turned to her father. "What are the boys doing?"

Looking at her over his glasses, he cleared his throat. "George, Robert, and Beth are up in the boys' room playing jacks where the little ones can't interfere, and Ben is over at John's house. Why?"

"No reason." Polly's voice went flat.

Mother's knitting needles flew as she glanced at Maggie reading on a stool near the stove. "Why don't you and Maggie play a game?"

"I don't feel like playing a game." Polly flopped down again on the dark green davenport beside her mother. She picked up the skein of yellow yarn Mother was turning into a baby blanket.

Wrinkling her brow, Mother opened her mouth but loud footsteps on the front porch interrupted. Father sprang up as someone knocked on the door.

He turned on the porch light and peered out the window. When he opened the door, Garrett stood there with his golden hair gleaming in the light. Polly's breath caught in her throat and she clapped her hand over her mouth.

Arms crossed, Polly's father stood in the doorway. "What can I do for you?"

Garrett held his head high, shoulders back, exuding confidence. "I came to ask if Polly wants to go for a sleigh ride. The weather is perfect."

Father gave Polly a long silent look, while her heart pounded so loud she was sure everyone in the room could hear it. She had so many questions for Garrett. "What about your girl friend?" and "Where have you been for the past four months?" or "Why should I?" But those questions didn't seem appropriate with her family in the room. At the same time, she *wanted* to say "yes" and get out of the house before her restlessness drove her crazy.

"Make up your mind, Polly. I'm letting in a lot of cold air."

Polly jumped up. "I'll go." She grabbed her coat from its hook on the wall, pulling out the warm green hat, gloves and scarf she kept stuffed in her pockets. It was too cold to worry about looking fashionable.

Father returned to his paper and Mother went on knitting. They were both frowning. Eyes wide, Elsie and Twila stared at Garrett. Even when he had come often, he never talked to Polly's sisters.

She hurried to the door to escape the deafening silence that hung in the room. Calling good-bye, she slammed the door behind her.

As Garrett approached his father's team of horses, they pawed the ground. They were snorting and blowing out big breathes that curled like steam from a teakettle into the crisp night air. When he offered his arm as Polly climbed into the sleigh, her eyes widened, surprised he actually made an effort to help her.

In spite of all her questions, Polly found herself tongue-tied now that she and Garrett were alone. She waited for him to say something. He spread a blanket over their laps and then clucked to the horses.

When the silence became more than awkward, both of them started to talk at once. "You first," Polly insisted. What would he say with no guidance from her?

Garrett looked at her. "I'm sorry I haven't been around for awhile, Polly. I've been busy with my new job in Mercer. It's quite a drive."

Polly's spine stiffened and she turned toward him, breathing hard. *"Don't lie to me."*

She had nursed her anger ever since her father had told her about Garrett's lies and deceptions, and now it roared into flame.

"I know you had other girl friends all the time you led me to believe you loved me, and I know you're courting someone else now."

"I never said I loved you, Polly, and we weren't engaged. You could have dated other men too. A person is only young once. I don't think it's wise to get serious too soon."

Polly rubbed her hands over her eyes. How did he do this to her? He always made her doubt herself, always made her believe she was being unreasonable. Things had seemed so clear when her father told her his concerns. Now, after just a few minutes of conversation, she felt confused and mixed up again.

"I just needed time." Garrett smoothed his hair. "Time to be sure you were the right one."

Giving her head a hard shake, Polly glared at him. "But I saw you with a girl a couple months ago. It looked like you were serious about her. Who is she?"

Garrett cleared his throat. "Savannah Stevens from Georgia. I *was* serious about her. Then I found out she wasn't what she pretended to be. She was just leading me on."

"Kind of like how you weren't what *you* pretended to be and just led *me* on?"

The question hung in the cold, crisp air. Then Garrett took Polly's mittened hand. "Ah, Pol..." He leaned toward her and tried to look into her eyes. "Don't be like that."

Polly pulled her hand away and refused to meet his eyes. "How did it feel to be on the receiving end, Garrett?"

He sat up straighter. "If that's the way you're going to be, I might as well take you home."

In spite of her resolution not to let Garrett beguile her, Polly didn't want to go back to the house. It had felt more and more like a prison as the winter wore on. She stared at Garrett. He had used her in the past when he wasn't serious about her. Maybe she could do the same. "I don't want to fight with you, Garrett. Let's just enjoy our sleigh ride and talk about something else."

His brows went up and his eyes widened. He shrugged. "All right by me."

Soon they were talking and laughing as they had in the past while the stars twinkled above them. Surely if she were careful, there could be no harm in being friends with Garrett even though she didn't trust him.

CHAPTER 25

"Will you pick up a few things at the market and also get the mail?" Mother's face was pale as she held out a list for Polly.

Twila and Elsie came running. "Go too, pwease?" Elsie batted her eyelashes at Polly.

"Not this time." Polly shook her head and took Mother's list. "I can't carry you *and* the groceries *and* the mail."

"Walk, Polly. We walk." Twila and Elsie clutched Polly's skirt.

Polly chuckled. "You say that now, but soon you'd be saying, 'Carry me. Carry me.' There's still some snow in the backyard. Maybe Maggie can take you out to play."

Glad for an excuse to walk to town, Polly couldn't blame the little ones for wanting to get out of the house. Everyone needed a break from being cooped up all winter.

Striding down Broad Street then turning right on Main, Polly soon reached the post office a quarter of a mile from their house. A gathering place for friends and neighbors, it was a good way to hear the latest news. She pushed open the door. A larger-than-usual group of people stood talking in hushed tones.

Polly greeted a few of them, then headed to the counter. The postmaster, William Boyd, would be the most reliable source of information. She smiled at Mr. Boyd. "What's going on?"

"Have you heard Kitt Potter is missing?"

"No, since when?"

"I believe she disappeared a few days ago, maybe Wednesday. No one has seen her since. Her mother is worried sick."

Polly frowned. Kitt had acted strange when she last visited Polly. What had they talked about?

Mr. Boyd leaned toward her. "What is it, Polly? Do you have an idea where Kitt might be?"

"No, I was just thinking of the last time I saw her. She acted a little odd."

"When was that?"

Polly wrinkled her forehead. "Right after Christmas."

"If you think of anything that might help, please tell her mother."

"Of course I will. Could I have our mail, please?"

Leaving the post office, Polly tripped on the last step. Physical culture—that was it. She and Kitt had talked about Physical Culture after Kitt asked to go into the sitting room and closed the door. So strange.

What else had she and Kitt talked about? Polly headed for the market. Kitt had seemed sad and so desperate to improve her figure. She had started to say she was writing to someone before she added, "I shouldn't have said anything. He said not to."

Who was "he?" And did he have anything to do with Kitt's disappearance? Or was Polly's imagination working overtime again?

Walking around the store, Polly picked up a small bag of sugar and a container of cocoa. Thank goodness she had a list or she wouldn't have remembered what to buy. When she went up to pay for her groceries, seven or eight people milled around at the front of the store. She heard Kitt's name. Nothing remained a secret long in a small town like Sandy Lake.

Polly didn't hear any new information and didn't say anything that would draw attention to herself. She shouldn't have said anything to Mr. Boyd. If Kitt had been keeping a secret, she wouldn't appreciate Polly giving it away. On the other hand, if she was in trouble, it might be better to disclose everything Polly knew.

She paid for her groceries and slipped out of the store, a rhythmic pounding starting behind her temples. This was the most excitement Sandy Lake had seen since Doc Cooley bought the first gas-powered car in their town, yet not the kind of excitement Polly preferred. Untrustworthy people and difficult situations affected her this way.

Garrett—speaking of untrustworthy people and difficult situations. Those words defined him and their relationship well. She walked faster.

As always, thinking about Garrett triggered imaginary conversations with her mother. Conversations to justify her behavior. She'd gone out with Garrett a couple more times since she went on the sleigh ride with him—nothing serious, no strings attached. Yet, each time she went, the looks her parents gave her became darker. Polly always assured them, "We're not serious."

She made it home in record time, trying to escape her thoughts. When Polly sprinted up the porch steps, her mother was looking out the window. She started speaking before Polly closed the door. "I heard a rumor about Kitt Potter."

"So did I. They were talking about her at the post office *and* at the market."

"Could you watch the girls? I want to see if Kitt's mother needs anything."

"Of course."

Mother reached for her "pregnant" coat, the one she always wore when her regular coat wouldn't button anymore. "She came to see you not long ago. Did she say anything that might help us find her?"

Polly squirmed under Mother's direct look. She shared her last conversation with Kitt, but before she reached the part about Kitt writing to someone, Mother broke in.

"Poor thing."

Polly bit her lip. "Kitt said..."

"It's a shame she's so unhappy in spite of all she has to be thankful for."

The hammering in Polly's right temple thumped harder. Maybe for now it was better to keep Kitt's secret.

As the days dragged on, all of Sandy Lake seemed to hold its breath. People speculated about Kitt's disappearance. Everyone was worried. Except for Garrett. He grunted and snorted whenever the subject came up. "She's a foolish young woman. She probably did something stupid. What difference does that make to me?"

"She's my friend, and it makes a difference to *me.*" Polly glared at him as he sat behind the wheel of his car with an arrogant lift to his chin. "Don't you ever think of anyone except yourself?"

Garrett's jaw hardened and he pulled on the accelerator lever. The car leapt forward.

I can't believe I just said that. I was going to keep my mouth shut.

♠

Polly stood on the front steps of the Potter's home. Would someone answer her knock? Would they be home on a Wednesday afternoon? What would she say if they answered? Minutes ticked by. Maybe Mrs. Potter and Bess had been hounded by well-meaning neighbors and friends, as well as information seekers, and weren't seeing anyone. Just as Polly started to turn away, the door opened a few inches.

"Oh, it's you, Polly." Mrs. Potter opened the door wider. "We've been trying to keep Kitt's disappearance out of the newspapers, so I wanted to be sure you weren't a reporter."

Polly cleared her throat. "No, but I have some information that might help."

"Please come in." Mrs. Potter motioned her inside.

Gazing at the glass chandeliers with sparkling pendants and love seats with gleaming velvet upholstery, Polly almost forgot her mission. These things must have cost a fortune. Mr. Potter must have made a lot of money in his mercantile business in Ohio and his involvement in the railroad. Yet none of these costly possessions had made Kitt happy, and none of them had the power to bring her back.

Mrs. Potter pointed to one of the loveseats. "Please sit down."

Polly perched on the edge. *Too beautiful to sit on.*

Settling on a chair across from her, Mrs. Potter leaned forward, eyes wide. "Am I to assume the information you have is about Kitt?"

"It is. Kitt came to see me after Christmas when I hurt my ankle."

"I remember."

"She talked about Physical Culture. Were you aware of her obsession?"

Kitt's mother waved her hand. "Oh my yes. Kitt was relentless in her pursuit of a better figure."

"She said the classes weren't helping and told me she'd been writing to someone. She wouldn't say who and said 'he' had told her not to say anything." Polly held her breath.

Mrs. Potter sighed. "I know Kitt wrote to someone who gave her advice about Physical Culture. She wouldn't tell *me* his name either." She rubbed her forehead. "I told her if he was legitimate, he wouldn't mind her telling me. But she wouldn't listen, and she's not a child anymore."

Polly squirmed. Her parents might be saying that about her and her relationship with Garrett. *"She won't listen to us, and she's not a child anymore."*

She rubbed her forehead and stood up. "I guess you already knew what I came to tell you. Do you have any idea where Kitt might be?"

Mrs. Potter followed Polly as she walked across the gold-bordered burgundy area rug. "No idea at all. Her big brother, Seymour, offered to come home, but what could he do? We don't have any clues. And if she went of her own free will, I don't know if she even wants to come home."

"I'm so sorry, Mrs. Potter."

"Thank you for coming. I know your mother's praying for Kitt's safe return."

"God answers my mother's prayers. Surely you'll hear something soon."

With a heavy heart, Polly headed home. *She wouldn't listen to me, and she's not a child anymore.* She stuffed her fingers in her ears but couldn't drown out the words.

As she entered their cozy living room, Mother looked up from her knitting. "Where were you? I thought you'd gone upstairs."

"I talked to Mrs. Potter."

"Any news about Kitt?"

Polly shook her head, relaying her conversation with Kitt's mother as she removed her coat and stripped off her boots.

"*You* knew Kitt had been writing to someone?"

"Yes, I tried to tell you the other day. Kitt wouldn't say who it was." Polly hung up her coat and scarf.

"That doesn't sound good." Mother frowned, and then sighed. "I'm sure Catherine tried to talk to her, but Kitt's not a child anymore."

Those words again. Polly wanted to cover her ears to shut out her mother's voice as she had years ago. Instead, she murmured, "No she's not, and whatever happens, she will have only herself to blame." The words sounded ominous, even to her.

CHAPTER 26

Maggie burst through the door, mail in hand, shouting, "Mrs. Potter had a letter from Kittie today. Well, sort of a letter."

"What do you mean—*sort of a letter*?" Polly asked as she and Mother hurried in from the kitchen.

"It was written on a piece of a sugar bag and postmarked Atlantic City, New Jersey. I saw it myself when Mr. Boyd handed it to Mrs. Potter. She was shaking so hard, Mrs. Smith had to read it to her. It said something like this: *I am in a trap. I wish I had taken mother's advice. I feel like jumping into the ocean to end it all.*"

"Oh my." Perspiration broke out on Polly's forehead. Could this scenario get any worse?

"What will they do?" Mother sat down heavily on the couch, wiping her eyes with her dishtowel.

"Mrs. Potter said she's going to send Seymour to Atlantic City to hire a detective."

"All right then." Mother nodded. "We can ask God to send His angels to help Seymour and the detective find her."

What could have happened to cause Kitt to be so desperate? Polly conjured up awful circumstances. All because she hadn't taken her mother's advice. Polly stiffened. *It's not the same as me going out with Garrett. Besides, a person can't spend her whole life doing what her parents say. At some point, she has to make her own decisions.*

♠

The phone broke the early morning stillness on Wednesday. Polly turned over in bed and yawned. Who could be calling at this hour? Mother's low voice drifted up the stairs but she couldn't make out the words.

Half an hour later, still unable to sleep, curiosity drove Polly from her bed. She stumbled down the stairs, the fragrance of coffee growing stronger. Mother sat in her favorite chair with her Bible open in her lap, coffee cup in hand. The morning light glinted from the leaded windowpane and glowed on her face.

"Who called?"

Mother smiled. "Good morning to you, too. Catherine Potter called to tell us Seymour and the detective found Kittie in Atlantic City last night. They'd been searching almost nonstop since Seymour arrived."

"Why did Kitt go to Atlantic City?"

"Catherine didn't seem to want to talk about it. She said Seymour and Kittie should be home tomorrow night."

"Maybe there'll be details in the paper." Polly hugged herself and shivered. "How embarrassing to have the whole world talking about your foolish mistakes."

"Not the whole world. She'll likely make headlines in the Greenville Evening Record and the Pittsburgh papers though. Maybe even some of the larger newspapers on the east coast."

Polly cringed. "What was Kitt *thinking*, going to Atlantic City alone?"

Her mother shook her head. "Young people sometimes make foolish decisions when they're trying to assert their independence."

"But how are we ever to become adults unless we assert our independence?"

"Only by learning to be guided by the Holy Spirit and not by our own desires and schemes." Polly's mother stood, patted her shoulder and walked away.

What did that mean? How could a person be guided by the Holy Spirit? She sighed. So much to learn.

She drummed her fingers on the back of Mother's chair. Why couldn't they have a morning paper like most towns? *Shame on you for being so eager to read about your friend's scandal. What kind of friend are you?*

What should a friend do at a time like this? Why was it so hard to find the right words to pray? She knew Mother was praying. Maybe that was enough. Maybe she should try to visit Kitt when she came home. As Polly started upstairs to get dressed, she dismissed the idea. Kitt probably wouldn't want to speak to anyone.

The day dragged as Polly helped get the children off to school. She entertained Twila and Elsie while Mother cleaned up after breakfast. Lunch came and went, and finally in the late afternoon, Polly heard the thud she'd been waiting for. She opened the door and grabbed the newspaper that had landed reasonably close to the entrance today.

She scanned the front-page headlines. Nothing about Kitt. She turned a page, then another. There was the headline on page four. *GIRL TELLS COURT OF FAKE DOCTOR'S POWER.* Impressed that the family had managed to keep the biggest news in Sandy Lake off the front page, Polly read on. *Cut Her Hair and Dressed Her in Boys' Clothes to Avoid Police Raid, She Asserts—Dr. is Held on Two Serious Charges.* The story was dated April 13, 1911, Atlantic City.

Although there were no pictures, Polly's vivid imagination filled in the details. Kitt standing before the court, brother at her side, beautiful braids gone, hair cropped short, dressed as a boy from the waist up—the court matron had loaned her a skirt. In monosyllables, she testified Dr. Girard had forced her to live in a tent with him. He said their tent would be raided if she didn't agree to the disguise.

Polly groaned and dropped into a chair as she stared at the paper. Mother came into the room carrying Twila. "Is Kittie's story in the newspaper?"

"On page four."

"Does it say why she went to Atlantic City?"

"She saw Doctor Girard's Physical Culture advertised in the newspaper. Since she was dissatisfied with her slight figure and wanted to be more beautiful, she wrote to him. It says forty letters written by Girard were offered as exhibits. "

"Forty letters." Mother's face turned pink. "That scoundrel. I wonder what he said to convince her."

"He assured her the lessons were on 'a high moral plane.' "

"Indeed." Mother snorted and Twila patted her cheek. "If the lessons were on a high moral plane, there'd have been no reason to keep them secret." Mother's brown eyes sparked. "They should lock that man up and throw away the key. I bet it isn't the first time he's pulled a scheme like this."

Polly ran her finger down the newspaper column. "It says they found more than five hundred letters written by Girard to girls of moneyed families in all sections of the country."

"I'm surprised he didn't try to get a ransom from the family. Poor Kittie. I don't know if she'll ever get over this." Mother paused, then came and sat down beside Polly and looked her in the eye. "I'm so sorry for what Kitt is going through, but I do hope you're learning what terrible consequences can come from just one poor choice."

Dropping her gaze, Polly reached for Twila who had been squirming. "Let's go read some stories while Mother makes dinner." She frowned at her mother. "I'm not about to run off to Atlantic City because some fake doctor says I should. I'm not that stupid."

Mother opened her mouth, then closed it again. As Polly walked away, she thought she heard her murmur, "She's not a child..."

♠

Polly tossed and turned all night. Vivid mental pictures of Kitt and the infamous Dr. Girard made sleep impossible. She tried not to disturb her younger sisters. Today was Saturday and they wouldn't thank her if she awakened them early. If she had a room of her own, she could light a lamp.

Finally, she got up, pulled on her robe and slippers and went downstairs. Even though they were halfway through April, the house still got chilly at night. It looked like Father had already put another log on the fire. As she lit the small gas lamp on the table, she noticed the hook by the door. His coat and hat were gone. Where would he have gone so early on a Saturday? He and Ben weren't working in the mine today.

Pulling the warm knitted afghan from the back of the divan, Polly snuggled up and closed her eyes. Over and over she willed herself to sleep. She must have dozed because she jerked awake when the front door creaked and Father came in.

"Where were you?" Polly yawned and rubbed the sleep from her eyes, just as her father asked, "What are you doing up so early?"

"I couldn't sleep. What about you?"

"I couldn't sleep either." Father laid some newspapers on the table and slipped off his hat and coat. "I went to see if the Pittsburgh papers were in."

"Why?"

"I can't stop thinking about Kittie Potter. I wanted to see if today's papers had anything new."

"Did you find anything?"

"She got home yesterday, early evening. The family said they wanted privacy, so Catherine waited alone for Kittie and Seymour at the train station. One of the papers had a statement given by her mother. It said Kitt doesn't want to talk to anyone."

Father spread the newspapers on the table, and Polly came to lean down beside him. Together they read from the Gazette Times.

My daughter greatly regrets her experience and is glad to be back home again. Katherine says she was unable to control her actions for the greater part of the time, due to the hypnotic influence this man had over her, and that even now, distance and time considered, she is still somewhat under the spell.

Father cleared his throat. "Part of the headline in the Pittsburgh Daily Post said: *Miss Potter, Who It is Claimed, Was Hypnotized, Refuses to Issue Statement.*"

Polly squinted at her father. "Do you believe that?"

"Do I believe Kittie was hypnotized?" Father shook his head. "Not in the technical sense. But perhaps there's more than one way to be hypnotized."

"What do you mean?"

"If someone is eloquent or a smooth talker, they might convince people to do things they ordinarily wouldn't. Technically, those people aren't hypnotized, but they act as though they are." Father paused. He gazed at Polly. "For example, Garrett..." Then he closed his mouth and shook his head.

Polly stood up straight. "If you're trying to say I'm hypnotized by Garrett, you're wrong. I'm only seeing him because my life is boring without him. When I went out with him before, he was using me, so now it's my turn."

Her father's dark brows drew together and his brown eyes became dark pools. "Florence Dye, nothing good ever came of returning evil for evil."

CHAPTER 27

Garrett walked down the porch steps and headed for his car. The weather grew warmer each day. Some of the spring flowers were blooming, or at least in bud, as they neared the middle of May. His mood did not match the weather. He was grumpy and out of sorts. His life had been dull since he'd learned the truth about Savannah.

He cranked his car and got in to go to work. For the first time, he was unable to put a girl behind him at will. His reflex reaction had been to revive his relationship with Polly. But even though they had fun, he had no feelings for her.

Garrett's trips to work had lost their appeal. Even driving wasn't as much fun as it used to be. In spite of his anger and determination to end the relationship, he looked for Savannah every time he drove through Jackson Center. Twice he'd been on the verge of stopping, then changed his mind when he'd seen Mr. Sullivan walking down the sidewalk.

Polly's mother would probably say that was God's way of reminding him of why he had broken up with Savannah. He snorted. *Right. Like God cared about things like that.* Garrett believed in God—sort of—but did God want to be involved in his life personally? He didn't think so. Regardless, Garrett wanted to be in charge of his own life. He wanted to decide whether or not he'd see Savannah again. It was *his* choice.

♠

As Polly walked down Broad Street enjoying the sunshine, she studied the Potter residence. She hadn't seen Kitt since the episode in Atlantic City. When Kitt's face appeared at one of the multi-colored glass squares in the front door, Polly raised her hand to wave. Kitt opened the door and called, "Would you like to come in?"

Polly's eyes widened. "Of course." She hurried up the steps.

As Kitt swung the door wide, Mrs. Potter smiled and greeted her. Kitt motioned for Polly to follow her upstairs. "Let's go to my room."

Maybe Kitt wanted to talk. She had never invited her to come upstairs. Polly was so afraid of saying the wrong thing. She'd heard Kitt didn't want to talk about her misfortune. Should she ask how she was doing? If only Mother were here, she'd know what to say. Even though she didn't like Mother giving her advice, she trusted her mother's judgment in situations like this.

Kitt ushered Polly into her bedroom, and she looked around the lovely room. The Trip Around the World quilt on Kitt's double bed, where she slept *alone*, had feminine shades of lavender and pink material which matched the curtains at her windows. What would it be like to sleep alone instead of three in a bed?

She brushed her hand over her eyes. Why should she be envious when none of this had made Kitt happy?

As Polly sat on the corner of Kitt's spacious feather bed, her friend plopped down beside her. Taking a deep breath, Polly gazed at her. "How are you doing? Are you going to be okay?"

"I don't know if I'll ever be okay." Kitt shrugged. "I'm so embarrassed. How would you like to have the whole town gossiping about your mistakes? I can't believe I was so stupid. Dr. Girard told me his 'high sense of professional honor' would be my protection. Some protection."

"I'm so sorry, Kitt. I should have tried harder to find out who you were writing to when you came to my house. Maybe I could have talked you out of going to Atlantic City."

"I doubt it. My mother tried to make me tell her who I was writing to, but I was so stubborn. And so desperate to improve my figure."

Polly smoothed the satiny quilt. "Had you ever met Dr. Girard?"

"No, he said he'd wear a red carnation in his buttonhole so I'd recognize him after I took the midnight train to Atlantic City."

"Didn't you wonder about all the secrecy?"

"He convinced me it was all necessary for his treatment to work. He took me to a hotel on Atlantic Avenue for the first one."

"What kind of treatment?"

"He called it all Physcultopathy." Kitt buried her face in her hands. "It... It... He..." She sobbed aloud. "Oh, I can't bear to talk about it."

"It's okay. You don't have to."

Kitt drew a long, shuddering sob. "After my treatment, he wouldn't leave." She lifted her face and tears rolled down her cheeks. Polly's heart contracted.

"He said improvement could only come when I was within the radius of his pschyophatic influence. I was so frightened. He stayed all night." Kitt sniffled. "One of the newspapers said I was an 'unsuspecting, unsophisticated country girl' and they were right. Stupid, stupid, stupid."

Polly put her arm around Kitt's quaking shoulders and stroked her short, shaggy brown hair.

"Whenever I talked about leaving, he'd say, 'Oh, very well, then; we'll both be arrested. It won't hurt me, but it'll hurt you.' I believed him."

Polly's stomach churned. The phony doctor had played on Kitt's timidity and fears. "The paper said he made you live in a tent under 'the figure eight.' What's that?"

"It's a huge roller coaster opposite Young's Million Dollar pier. The professor said we had to live outdoors for the treatment to be effective. He watched me all the time. When I tried to escape, he tracked me down. People were starting to get suspicious of us living together in the tent, so he started calling me Jack, cut my hair and made me wear boy's clothes."

Polly hugged Kitt. "It's all over. He's in jail and can't hurt you now."

"It isn't over. I still have to testify at his trial in June. I don't want him to do this to anyone else." Kitt pulled a lacey handkerchief out of her pocket and blew her nose. "And I don't know how long he'll be in jail. My lawyer says he might get off easy since he didn't kidnap me. I'm an adult and I went willingly. Stupid. Stupid. Stupid."

Patting Kitt's trembling hands, Polly opened and closed her mouth. What should she say? What would Mother say? She took a deep breath. "Kitt, even adults make mistakes and do things they regret. I've done some stupid things. Everyone has. What's important is that we learn from our mistakes and become wiser and more mature."

Hmm... Good advice, Polly. She hugged Kitt again.

Kitt sat up straight and clenched her fists. "I *know* I've learned from this mistake."

"I'm sure you have." Polly squeezed her friend's hand and stood up. "I'd better head for home. Mother might need me."

Kitt held onto Polly's fingers. "Your mother's going to have a baby, isn't she?"

"Sometime in August. The heat of summer will be hard on her."

"Your mother is one of the wisest people I know. I envy you."

This was the second time Kitt had said she envied her—words she'd never expected to hear from Kitt even once.

After Kitt saw her out, Polly sprinted down the road and up the steps to her house. *There's no comparison between dating Garrett just for fun and Kitt meeting a stranger in Atlantic City. Garrett is no stranger. I know exactly what he's like—he doesn't have me fooled for a minute.*

Stepping across the threshold, Polly had a chill of apprehension in spite of the warm sunshine. *Just like the day we moved in more than a year ago.* How carefree and exuberant she had been that day until this same unwelcome feeling had quenched her excitement.

That was before Garrett had broken her heart. Even her anger at him couldn't distract her from the apprehension that clung to her.

Polly tried to analyze the feeling. The oppression seemed to emanate from the back bedroom where Mother and Father slept. She had never mentioned her misgivings to her mother, always certain she would think Polly was being silly.

Twila came running as Polly stood by the door. She scooped her up in her arms. Eventually, she would have to read the last few pages of Sarah's dairy. She couldn't keep avoiding the let down that seemed inevitable. Especially if it held no answers to her questions.

Giving herself a strong mental shake, Polly went in search of Mother. She was in the kitchen as usual, heating soup for lunch. "Do you need help?"

Mother smiled as she tried to bend over to tie Elsie's shoe. Her protruding abdomen made it difficult. Polly gently took her place.

"There's always something to do. Where were you? Out getting some sunshine?"

"I took a walk, and Kitt invited me to come in. We went up to her room. She told me what happened in Atlantic City. Come sit down and I'll tell you about it."

Mother looked at the soup. "Maybe just for a minute."

As they sat at the table, Mother cautioned her. "Be careful what you say in front of the girls."

"I don't think they're old enough to understand, but I'll be careful."

As Polly related the things Kitt had told her, Mother kept shaking her head. "If there's anything I can't stand, it's unscrupulous people taking advantage of innocent women and children. And he might get off with a lighter sentence because she's an adult?"

Mother's lovely brown eyes filled with tears as she stood and started toward the kitchen. "That's just wrong. In no time at all, he'll be out hoodwinking some other innocent young woman."

CHAPTER 28

With lunch behind them and both little girls tucked in for a nap, Polly convinced her mother to lie down. Free for now, Polly rummaged in her bureau drawer, her latest hiding place for Sarah's diary. She tucked it under her apron and scooted down the stairs.

She hesitated. Should she stay indoors in case the girls needed her? Their sleepy chatter had quieted a few minutes ago and the sunshine drew her. With one last look up the steps, she headed for the door. Plopping down on the edge of the porch, she savored one more moment of anticipation and opened the diary.

December 1, 1893. Harry and Blanche have gotten married and are living out at McCuthison Run on Potter's Farm. Even though Harry and his sister, Naomi, have always used the name "Davis," Harry had to use "Whitman," his legal name, on their marriage license.

Harry and Blanche Davis. The names were familiar. The people who lived next door were named Harry and Blanche. They had brought Polly's family a pie when they first moved in. Was their last name Davis? Could Harry be Sarah's grandson? Polly's cheeks flushed and her pulse quickened.

Yesterday God granted one of my dearest desires. I held my first great grandson soon after he was born. My health has been so poor, I didn't think I'd live to see his face. Harry and Blanche named him Vance after our son, Richard Vance. RV was so honored. If I didn't worry so much about Nancy, I'd be happy to go home to glory now. I'm so eager to see my Lord whom I've loved and served so long.

Sarah's handwriting looked more and more shaky. Polly turned the page.

None of my family wants to hear this, but I know I don't have much time left. Since they're reluctant to call a lawyer, acknowledging that my time is near, I've decided to write my wishes here. I've read some wills that lawyers have prepared, so I'll try to use the same wording and trust it will be legal.

Polly squinted at the spidery handwriting that was, apparently, Sarah's last will and testimony:

First, I commend my soul to God in whom I put my trust. Second, as to such worldly possessions as God has seen fit to entrust to my care and keeping, I dispose as follows:

I direct that my real estate should remain in the possession of my husband, Thomas Davis, during his natural life and at his death, it should go to my two sons, William T. Davis and Richard Vance Davis to be held by them in fee sample, free of encumbrances.

Did that mean Sarah didn't have any debts on her real estate?

Second, I direct that at my death, my personal property should be divided equally between my two sons, William T. Davis and Richard Vance Davis, share and share alike.

What about Nancy? Polly frowned. Weren't girls allowed to inherit in those days? On the other hand, perhaps, her mental condition was so poor she wouldn't have been capable of being responsible for anything Sarah might entrust to her.

Lastly, I appoint my sons, William T. Davis and Richard Vance Davis, as my executors in carrying out my last will and testimony.

The next entry was the last one in the journal. Polly paused, took a deep breath, then read on.

March 4, 1894. I'm growing weaker every day. Blanche has promised that after my death, she'll put my diary back in its hiding place. It seems strange, but I believe that's what God wants me to do.

Dr. Cooley says the condition of my lungs will cause my death, even though for years I've thought it would be my heart. In spite of all he can do, pneumonia has an unrelenting hold on me. My fever has been so high that Thomas says I'm completely out of my head at times. Nighttime is the worst.

Last night my family agreed to copy what I'd written in this book as my will. My hands shook so much, I just made my mark instead of signing my name. Nancy carried on so bad I fear for her sanity. How will Thomas manage when I'm gone? Harry and Blanche have built a small house next door so perhaps they'll help.

Sarah's grandson and his wife had built a house beside Sarah's house. They must be the same Harry and Blanche who still lived there. All the while she'd been reading Sarah's diary, they'd been right next door. Maybe Blanche could tell her if something bad had happened in this house.

Polly turned back to read the last few words.

Father, I've always put my trust in you. If only I had...

Surely Sarah was addressing her heavenly Father in that last line... What had she been about to write?

CHAPTER 29

It had been hard to fall asleep last night knowing Sarah's relatives lived next door. Could Polly talk to them soon?

Scurrying down the stairs, she found Mother hunched over the dining room table. She stepped closer. "Good morning, Mother."

Mother glanced at her, face pale and haggard as she sat there alone. Maybe the dim light of the gas lamp was to blame.

Polly studied her. "How did you sleep last night?"

"I was..." Mother paused. "I was restless and uncomfortable. It seems something isn't quite right with this baby, though I can't say what the problem is. I don't feel like I did with my other babies. I've been spotting a little, too."

"I think you've been working too hard. Should I call Dr. Cooley?"

"No, no. This isn't an emergency. You know how busy he's been. I doubt there'd be anything he could do."

"Just rest here while I make breakfast. I'll fetch Twila first before she wakens Elsie."

Not waiting for a response, Polly started up the stairs. Twila's sleepy early morning noises increased in volume.

By the time Polly reached the nursery, Twila was standing in her crib staring at the doorway. She kissed the little girl in her white cotton nightgown and gathered her close, smelling her sweet baby scent.

Twila snuggled her head against Polly's shoulder. Polly choked on the lump in her throat. *I have to take care of this baby.*

Unable to understand her emotions, Polly tightened her grip on the vulnerable child and hurried downstairs.

In the kitchen, Mother busied herself with adding fragrant maple syrup to the oatmeal. Polly frowned, seeing Mother's unhealthy pallor. "Mother, come sit at the table with Twila, and I'll finish the oatmeal."

Mother opened her mouth, then rubbed her eyes and did as Polly suggested. "Did you bring Twila's clothes? I can get her dressed."

"Not yet. I didn't want to wake Elsie. I'll get Twila a cracker."

"Cracker, cracker." Twila beamed.

Mother sighed and sat beside Twila, resting her right elbow on the table and her head on her hand. The little girl's mouth turned down as she watched her mother.

Polly handed her sister a cracker and patted her head. "Mother will be all right. She just needs a little rest."

Was she reassuring herself or her sister? If only Father were here. She was used to handling things when Mother didn't feel well, but today the responsibility of dealing with Mother's condition weighed heavy on her young shoulders.

At last the oatmeal, jelly and toast were ready. Laughter and childish voices drifted down the stairs. If Polly didn't intervene, the other children would be bouncing on their beds and getting way too excited. She had loved doing that as a child, but she couldn't allow it today with Mother's fragile condition. Going to the foot of the stairs, she called, "Get dressed and come down for breakfast. Everything is ready. Maggie, please help Elsie, and bring some clothes for Twila."

Polly returned to the dining room where Twila had crumbled her cracker into miniscule pieces that dribbled down her nightgown onto the floor. Mother sat beside her with eyes closed, arms cradled over her abdomen. A splinter of fear stirred in Polly's heart. Why didn't Mother notice Twila's need for supervision?

"Mother?" Polly touched her mother's shoulder.

Mother's brown eyes opened, then closed again.

Leaning toward her, Polly tried to penetrate her lethargy. "Can you eat something?"

"No." Mother shook her head. "I'd better lie down."

"Do you want to lie on the couch?"

"No, upstairs. I don't want to frighten the little ones."

Polly helped her to her feet. Supporting Mother with one arm around her waist, they walked into the front room. Then one step at a time, they trudged up the stairs.

Elsie's high-pitched voice came from the bedroom at the top of the stairs where Maggie must have taken her. Snatches of Robert and George's arguing in the next room came through loud and clear. On a normal day, Polly loved these sounds. If only this were a normal day.

"Mother, will the baby will be all right?"

"I don't know. I've never felt this way before."

As they reached Mother's bedroom, Polly blew out a long breath. Gently she helped her sit on the edge of the bed and then recline, fluffing the pillows under her head and easing one under her knees. "Is there anything else I can get you?"

Mother closed her eyes and gave an almost imperceptible shake of her head. Polly shifted from one foot to the other, torn between wanting to stay with her mother and knowing there was nothing else she could do.

Her brothers' and sisters' footsteps clattered down the stairs rousing her. She had other responsibilities. But even though her feet hurried down the stairs, her heart remained at her mother's side.

Polly filled bowls with cereal for her siblings, while shushing them as she went back to the kitchen for bread and butter. "Mother isn't feeling well. Try not to disturb her."

"What's wrong with her?" George's tender heart, often hidden, was exposed in his worried brown eyes.

"I'm not sure. Sometimes she just needs extra rest." Polly didn't want to worry the other children with more details than they needed. *If only I could be shielded from the details.*

Maggie deposited Elsie onto a chair and came to where Polly buttered the toast. She lowered her voice. "What's really going on with Mother?"

Polly chewed her lip, then explained the situation.

Pressing her hands together, Maggie stood up tall. "I'm going to get Father. He'll know what to do."

"That's a wonderful idea." Polly hugged her. "But it's a long walk to the mine."

"I don't care."

Within minutes, Maggie had gulped her oatmeal and started for the door.

"Where's she going?" Robert scowled at Maggie's back.

"I'm going to get Father so he can decide whether Mother needs the doctor."

"If anyone should go for Father, it should be me." Robert tried to deepen his adolescent voice. "I'm the oldest man here when Ben and Father are at the mine."

Polly hid a smile as Robert's voice squeaked. "I appreciate your offer, but I'll need you to chop some wood soon so I can bake bread."

The scowl eased. "I'll go and take a look at the stove right now." Robert knocked his chair over in his eagerness.

"What about me? I'm learning to fix the fire, too." George glared at his brother.

"Next time, George. You can help next time. Go ahead, Maggie." Polly nodded at her sister. "Just be careful—and hurry."

As the door closed, Polly turned back to the dining room to meet the wide-eyed stares of the other children. "Now, all of you eat your breakfast. It won't do to let this food go to waste. You know Mother would want you to eat every bite."

The children visibly relaxed as Polly took charge, and within minutes, they were chattering as they ate. Polly collapsed in her chair. *Now that I've comforted the children, who will comfort me?*

CHAPTER 30

Polly paced back and forth across the little brown room adjoining her parents' bedroom. The minutes dragged as Dr. Cooley checked Mother for the second time. This morning, he'd thought she might be in premature labor but acknowledged there was very little he could do. He'd asked Polly to keep her mother as comfortable as possible. She bathed her face with cool water, rearranged her pillows, and brought her toast and juice or tea all day.

What was taking Doc so long? He had asked Father to join him in Mother's room without inviting Polly. Did he still think of her as a child?

The nursery seemed empty without her little sisters. Polly shivered. Father had moved Twila's crib into the room her older sisters shared, and Elsie would be sleeping in the big feather bed with Maggie and Blanche. It wouldn't do to have the little ones disturbed by all the activity in the back bedroom. For now, Polly would sleep in the new full-size bed Father had bought for Twila and Elsie to use after the new baby came.

Finally, the bedroom door opened and Father and Dr. Cooley came into the nursery. Father motioned to Polly. "You can go in now."

Polly stood her ground when Father stepped aside to let her enter. She did not intend to let them dismiss her so easily. She looked from Father to Dr. Cooley. "How is Mother doing? Do you think she's in labor?"

"I don't think so." The white-haired doctor shook his head. "The baby isn't due for about two months. I'm hopeful if your mother stays in bed for a few weeks, we may be able to postpone delivery."

"School is almost out." Father peered at Polly. "With Maggie's help, you should be able to take care of the house and the children. The boys can run errands for Mother."

Nodding, Polly entered her parents' bedroom. She stumbled, then kicked aside the rug that covered the loose board where she'd found Sarah's diary. The board creaked as it had the first day she'd entered this room. The apprehension it brought now tightened all her muscles and darkened the last rays of sunlight coming through the window. Why had she ever wanted this room as her own?

"What was that?" Dr. Cooley peered into the bedroom. Polly pushed past him and Father. She knew she should stay with Mother, but she couldn't stand the dark foreboding that seemed to fill the back bedroom. She fled from the nursery and down the stairs.

Children's voices and clattering of silverware came from the dining room where Maggie and the others were finishing supper. The last thing Polly wanted was food. Could she force something down? As she hesitated in the living room, someone knocked on the door.

Glad for the interruption, Polly sped to answer it. Blanche Davis's colorful scarf was visible through the window. Would this be her opportunity to ask if something bad had happened in this house?

Polly opened the door. "Come in. I'm sorry we haven't been very good neighbors."

Mrs. Davis patted Polly's arm. "I've spoken to your mother a number of times at the market. I don't know how I'd manage if I had eight children. Of course, she has you to help her. Your mother told me what a wonderful blessing you are to her."

Polly beamed. "I try to help all I can, especially now with another baby on the way."

"That's why I came." Mrs. Davis pointed out the window. "I heard Dr. Cooley's car pull up earlier. Is everything okay? Last time I saw your mother, she looked exhausted."

"I've been worried about her, too." Polly wrinkled her forehead. "Dr. Cooley was afraid she might be in premature labor. She'll have to be on bed rest for awhile."

As she spoke, Father and Dr. Cooley came into the room. Mrs. Davis smiled at them. "When is the baby due?"

Dr. Cooley raised an eyebrow at Father, who nodded. "Sometime in early August."

"Oh dear. That's still two months away."

"Yes, too soon." Dr. Cooley nodded and started for the door. He hesitated. "Blanche, perhaps you could help spread the word to the neighbors to bring in food while Margaret is unable to work."

Father shook his head. "I'm sure we can manage—"

"Bob, Margaret has many friends." Dr. Cooley set his jaw. "They'll want to help her, just as she would help them if they were in need."

Running his fingers through his hair, Father sighed. "Thanks, Doc."

When Mrs. Davis took a few steps toward the door, Polly put out her hand. "Mrs. Davis..."

"Please call me Blanche."

"Blanche, I've wanted to ask you some questions." Mrs. Davis's eyes widened as Polly turned to her father. "Are you going to stay with Mother for awhile?"

"Yes. I want to see how she's feeling."

Polly nodded toward the sitting room. "Do you have time to talk with me?"

"Of course. Anything I can do to help."

"Florence, what..." Father's forehead wrinkled in a puzzled frown, then he shook his head and started toward the steps. Polly followed Mrs. Davis into the sitting room.

Closing the door behind her, Polly sat down on Mother's small sofa and Mrs. Davis joined her. "Mrs—I mean, Blanche, did something bad happen in this house after Sarah Davis died?"

Blanche's mouth dropped and Polly winced. Did she always have to be so direct?

"What makes you think something bad happened here?"

"The day we moved in, I sensed something like a chill of apprehension when I stepped inside the door. I didn't know whether something bad had happened or if it was a premonition of something bad to come. It seems like I sense it most when I'm upstairs in the back bedroom."

Blanche's eyes took on a far away look as she settled on the sofa. "Harry's grandmother was a wonderful woman who had strong faith in God."

"Yes, I learned that from Sarah's diary. I found it soon after we moved in."

"I should have known. Before she died, Sarah asked me to put it back in its hiding place in Vance's room. She thought God had a plan for someone to find it." Blanche touched Polly's hand. "I guess it was you."

God had planned for her to find Sarah's diary?

"If you read her diary, you know she suffered many losses. I believe she lost five of her nine children before I met her."

Polly nodded and clenched her hands in her lap.

"Sarah survived but was very protective of her remaining children. Robert, or RJ, as most people called him, and Elizabeth were the only two who gained a measure of independence."

Closing her eyes, Blanche paused. "Sarah's daughter, Nancy, was the first casualty after Sarah's death."

She opened her eyes and stared out the window. "It was March 4, 1894. I'll never forget that day. I stood by the foot of the bed holding little Vance and watching as Sarah struggled to breathe. Thomas and their children surrounded the bed. We all knew Sarah's death was imminent. Nancy had been wailing off and on all day."

"Did your pastor come?"

"Reverend Long came earlier to pray with the family but that seemed to agitate Nancy even more. Maybe it made her mother's approaching death more real."

Polly leaned forward. "Was anyone else there?"

Blanche nodded. "My Harry. Thomas and Sarah had raised him and his sister since he was a baby. He was so devoted to his grandparents." Blanche wiped a tear from her cheek and bit her lip.

"What about his sister, Naomi?"

"Naomi had married and moved to California with her husband. An amazing feat, considering how dependent Sarah's children had been. If Naomi had been there, it might have helped to have another woman provide some comfort for Nancy. Her brothers and Harry meant well, but they lacked the nurturing gene."

"It must have been hard for you, trying to take care of your baby and comfort your sister-in-law." Polly touched Blanche's arm.

"So hard." Blanche clasped her hands. "When Nancy began to wail again, Vance, or RV, as we had taken to calling him since Harry named our son after him, came and took his namesake from me. He said Nancy's wailing was getting under his skin and asked if I'd talk to her."

Blanche stood and walked to the window. "I have to admit I didn't want to do it. Nothing I said seemed to help until I told her she'd have to be quiet if she wanted to stay in the room."

"How did she respond?" Polly stood and joined Blanche at the window.

"Her wild eyes calmed a bit and she seemed to comprehend what I was saying, but then Thomas spoke. *I think she's gone.* His voice wavered and then grew stronger. *Her suffering is over and she's at home with her Savior.*"

"Nancy pushed her father out of the way and rushed to her mother's side screaming, *No! No! Come back, Mama. Please come back. What will I do without you? Don't take her away from me, God. Please don't take her away.*"

CHAPTER 31

"Oh, Blanche, how awful! What did you do?" Polly led Blanche back to the sofa, noting her tight lips and tearstained cheeks.

Blanche opened her eyes. "We called Dr. Cooley. He came to confirm Sarah's death and give Nancy a sedative. We hoped in due time she would adjust and begin functioning again, but that never happened. She withdrew more and more into herself and had desperate bouts of wild crying. In the past, Sarah had been the only one who could calm her down." Blanche drew a long breath.

"Finally, Thomas had no choice but to have Nancy admitted to Warren State Hospital. We all felt terrible and visited her as much as we could."

"That must have been so hard on all of you." Polly squeezed Blanche's hand. "Maybe that's the reason for the bad feeling I've sensed in this house."

Closing her eyes so tight her forehead turned into a mass of wrinkles, Blanche sighed. "Oh that was only the beginning."

"Something else happened?" Polly's heart sank and her pulse quickened.

"Not right away. Things got a little better after we didn't have to deal with Nancy every day, but William wasn't doing well either. He didn't eat or sleep much after his mother died. He wandered around like a lost sheep."

Gripping the arm of the couch, Blanche took a deep breathe. "Poor Thomas tried his best to help him. He had to do William's work in the orchard besides keeping the store going.

Although RV seemed okay at first, the worse William got, the more it seemed to affect RV."

Blanche opened her eyes. "The bright spot in our world was little Vance." The wrinkles in her forehead relaxed. "Three years after Sarah's death, our little girl, Edna, was born. Her sweet smiles and winsome ways gave us such joy."

As Blanche's eyes took on a far away look, Polly drew a deep breath and braced herself. "William continued to struggle, however, and lost a lot of weight because he couldn't bring himself to eat. Dr. Cooley didn't find any physical reason for his loss of appetite except his inability to recover from his mother's death.

"Finally some time in November of that year, William died. The death certificate just said, 'complicated.' So sad. That was the beginning of our walk through the valley of the shadow of death."

Polly's heart skipped a beat. "Are you sure you want to tell me about this?"

"Sarah would have wanted you to know." Blanche took a deep breath. "In August of the next year, my precious baby contracted flux. The watery, foul-smelling diarrhea soaked through Edna's diaper onto her nightgown and sheets at night. No matter how I tried, I couldn't soothe the terrible diaper rash constantly irritated by diarrhea."

Blanche rubbed her forehead. "Edna cried a lot at night. I'd often fall asleep sitting by her crib, trying to pick her up before she woke Harry. Fortunately, Little Vance seemed able to sleep through anything."

"You must have been so tired."

"I was exhausted and concerned for the baby I carried in my womb, grieving as the onslaught of flux ravished Edna's wee body. Her weight dropped every day. Every bit of nourishment she swallowed was lost as the disease took its toll."

"Oh Blanche. How heartbreaking for you. And you were pregnant."

Nodding, Blanche pulled a worn handkerchief out of her pocket and blew her nose. "Even though Dr. Cooley had told us flux was very contagious, none of us wanted to stay away from Edna. Her pitiful cries broke our hearts. Grampa Thomas held her and comforted her many hours of the day so I could sleep. I shouldn't have let him do it. He always seemed so strong, but he was eighty-three years old. Eventually, he also came down with flux, and he and Edna got weaker every day.

"I feared for Nancy's health as well since Thomas had visited her just before the flux hit him."

Blanche was quiet for so long that Polly touched her arm. "Are you okay?"

Opening her eyes, her neighbor looked at her with such sorrow that Polly dropped her gaze. She pressed her hand against her heart. "If this is too hard for you, Blanche, you don't have to tell me."

"I believe I do."

Taking a deep breathe, Blanche continued her sad story. "Edna died the next day. My beautiful baby was only two years old." She repressed a sob. "Thomas died less than a week later on August twenty-third. By then we knew Nancy had also contracted the disease. She died the middle of September."

Polly stifled a sob and pulled a handkerchief out of her pocket and wiped her eyes.

"No one else got sick, and the baby I carried seemed okay. Harry and I had each other and Little Vance, but RV seemed so lost. He was alone now in that big house. Some days he didn't even open the store. Only the birth of Harry Junior in November seemed to ease his pain."

Blanche got up and walked to the window again. "In less than six months, our new baby started coughing. Harry Sr. had begun to cough a week earlier, but he shook off the illness, while Harry Jr. grew worse and worse. Dr. Cooley called it whooping cough."

Covering her face with her hands, Polly peeked at Blanche between her fingers. She didn't want to hear any more.

"Once again I sat up at night, this time beside Harry Jr.'s crib. Every time, Junior gasped for breath, I snatched him up, patted his back and prayed he would avoid the convulsions and vomiting which often followed. The pounds fell away from his small frame just as they had from Edna's. Was I caught in some kind of surreal nightmare? First, Edna's endless, foul-smelling diarrhea and now the coughing, convulsions and vomiting."

Polly dropped her hands from her face and went to Blanche's side. Blanche didn't turn from the window, although her eyes were closed. "I didn't know how we would survive another death. How would Harry and I go on living if we lost another precious baby? Was this how Sarah felt when she lost one baby after another?

"And what would become of RV? The look in his eyes when he heard Harry Jr. cough. There was no doubt he was regressing. He talked to people no one else could see, especially his mother. Sometimes he talked about her as though she were just in the next room. I feared for his sanity."

The silence lengthened and Polly patted her arm. "Blanche?"

Nodding, Blanche opened her eyes. They walked together to the couch. Blanche's voice dropped to a whisper. "My sweet baby died on May 3rd. It seemed like the end of the world."

Blanche got up to pace again. "RV got worse and worse. He couldn't work or pay his bills. In the end, he wouldn't come out of his room. He either called for Sarah repeatedly or had conversations with her. I couldn't help him—I had to fight my own battle with depression and despair."

Polly's eyes filled with tears. "Oh Blanche..." What could she say to someone who had experienced losses worse than she could even imagine?

"Two weeks later, they took RV to Warren State Hospital where Nancy had been. A committee was appointed to have him declared a lunatic. RJ tried to fight it but wasn't successful." Blanche's voice trembled. "RV was in that miserable place four long years before he died. They sold the house at a sheriff's sale."

"Oh no—" Polly covered her face again. "I'm so sorry, Blanche. I shouldn't have asked you."

Blanche perched on the edge of the sofa. "It's the end of Sarah's story, not recorded in her diary. I needed to tell you."

"So what I'm sensing in RV's room is probably the lingering darkness of his despair in those last months." Polly spoke more to herself than to Blanche.

"I wouldn't be surprised if that were true."

"How awful for you and Harry." Polly took Blanche's hand and they sat in silence. Then Polly stood. "Just a minute. I'll be right back."

Taking the steps two at a time, Polly sprinted up to her room. Ignoring Maggie and the girls, she pulled Sarah's diary out of her drawer and ran downstairs.

Out of breath, Polly opened the diary to the last page. "Sarah lived a godly life, didn't she?" Blanche nodded. Polly trailed her finger across the page. "Yet her last words were, *Oh Father, I've always put my trust in you. If only I had...* What do you think she wanted to say?"

Blanche was quiet for a moment. "Sarah had strong faith in God—except when it came to trusting Him with her children. As she grew older, she realized she had allowed them to become too dependent on her." She plucked a piece of lint off her rose-colored skirt.

"Most of all, toward the end when Nancy was reacting so badly to Sarah's impending death, Sarah wished she had encouraged her children to depend on the Lord, rather than depending so much on her. In her last few years, Sarah tried to change—to encourage her children to pray about things rather than just giving them answers when they had problems."

What had Mother said about how young people could become independent? Polly wrinkled her brow. Something about the Holy Spirit?

"I think Sarah's changes made a difference with Harry and Naomi. However, for her own children, it was too late—their dependency on her was too engrained."

Polly looked back at the last page of the diary. "So you think Sarah wanted to say, *If only I had taught my children to put their trust in you, God*?"

"Yes, I do. Rather than having strong faith in God, her children only had strong faith in her. She was their rock, their anchor, and when she was gone, the foundation of their lives was gone as well."

Polly bit her lip, fighting anger at God for allowing all those bad things to happen to Sarah's children. "But they faced losses that would have shaken anyone, didn't they?"

"It's true, but remember the parable Jesus told about the man who built his house on a rock, and the man who built his house on sand? Storms came to each of them, only the outcome was different. The house built on the rock didn't fall because it had a strong foundation."

"What about you, Blanche? You lost two precious babies, as well as many others who were dear to you. How did you survive the storms?"

"Only by God's grace, and by learning from Sarah's mistakes. I wanted to know God as well as Sarah did, in spite of the errors she made with her children. Little by little, I learned to make God my Rock, the strength of my life—not Harry, not Sarah, not my own parents."

Blanche tapped the diary and looked straight into Polly's eyes "What about you, Polly? Who do you go to when the storms come?"

CHAPTER 32

Polly tossed and turned on Twila and Elsie's new bed. She was on night duty while Father slept downstairs on the couch. So far, Mother slept peacefully—much more so than Polly.

Every time she closed her eyes, Blanche Davis's sad story gripped her. So much of what Blanche had said about Sarah's children depending on her hit way too close to home. She tried again to remember exactly what Mother had said when she'd asked her how young people were to become adults unless they asserted their independence.

Although she couldn't remember, the words her neighbor had spoken earlier that day were clear. "Sarah had a strong faith in God, but her children only had a strong faith in her. She was their rock, their anchor, and when she was gone, the foundation of their lives was gone as well."

Polly squirmed on the new mattress. *Could that also be true of me?* What about the day she had seen Garrett with the breathtaking Savannah snuggled up beside him in his car? Whom had she run to? And the day she'd tumbled down the snowy hill and twisted her ankle? How had she responded? Had she ever, even once, thought to pray, to cry out to God?

She pulled her legs up into a fetal position. God was a shadowy figure out there somewhere in whom she believed. However, when trouble came, it was Mother to whom she turned. *That would be appropriate for a child, but at the age of nineteen, I should have progressed further.*

Sitting up, she lit the gas lamp she'd brought upstairs and pulled Sarah's diary from under her pillow. Opening it, Polly skimmed through some of the entries. One jumped out at her in bold strokes. *If I turn against God, to whom will I go for the comfort and strength I need to get through the days ahead?*

When she'd wrestled with those words in Sarah's diary, Reverend Caldwell's message during Advent had helped her accept, at least in theory, that God didn't always prevent or deliver us from pain. However, she hadn't taken the additional step of choosing God to be the One to whom she turned for comfort and strength.

Mother was her rock. Polly thought of God more as her mother's God than her own.

She stared at Sarah's journal. Polly had been baptized as an infant in the Jackson Center Presbyterian Church. So had all her brothers and sisters. She had faithfully attended Sunday School there. She'd heard Bible stories about Adam and Eve, Daniel, David, and many more. Also, stories about Jesus, His death and His resurrection. *So what was the difference between her mother's faith and her own?*

She gasped and dropped the diary. How had she missed it? Mother's faith was very personal, not just about Bible stories that happened a long time ago. She talked to God like she talked to Father, like she would talk to a dear, respected friend. Polly nodded. *That's the difference between her faith and mine.*

Drawing a deep breath, Polly opened her mouth to pray, then closed it again. Could she call God "Father" as her mother did? She had never called Him that before, but she wanted to. "Father," she whispered. She cleared her throat and began again. "Father, I'm sorry I've ignored you for so long. In Sunday school they told us you sent your son, Jesus, to die for our sins so we could have a relationship with you. I never understood what that meant. Mother has a relationship with you, and I want to have one too. You've done your part, now I want to do mine. Thank you, Jesus, for dying for my sins."

Wrestling with the anger she'd felt when Blanche told her what happened to Sarah's children after she died, Polly knelt beside the bed. She dropped her head on the worn patchwork quilt. "I still want to blame you for bad things that happen, Father." Sniffling, she wiped a tear that slid down her cheek. "It's hard not to be angry at you. Help me trust you and put my faith in you no matter what happens. I want you to be my Rock, my Anchor, and the foundation of my life."

Polly paused. She bowed her head again.

"I'm beginning to understand, Father, that although parents are given to us as a gift from you, you never intended they should be a substitute for you. Please forgive me for putting my mother in your place for so long. Help me not to do it anymore."

"Florence."

Polly stood and entered Mother's dark bedroom. "Do you need something, Mother?"

"I saw the light and wanted to be sure you were okay."

"Did it wake you? I was having trouble sleeping and lit the lamp so I could read."

"What were you reading?"

Polly hesitated, but the time had come to tell her mother about Sarah's diary. "I've been reading the diary of Sarah Davis, the woman who originally bought this land with her husband and then lived here with their family. I found it under a loose board in this bedroom."

Mother frowned. "Do you think you ought to be reading..."

"Sarah Davis believed God wanted someone to find it after she died. I think that person was me."

"Why?"

"It's a long story. We can talk about it later. Right now you should try to sleep." Maybe later she'd find the courage to share her very personal conversation with God.

"Do you remember when I asked you how we are ever to become adults unless we assert our independence?"

"I remember."

"What did you say, Mama?" Her childhood name for her mother slipped out.

Even in the dark bedroom, Polly could hear the smile in her mother's voice. "I said it's only by learning to be guided by the Holy Spirit and not just following our own desires and schemes."

"The Holy Spirit. Something else we need to talk about tomorrow."

"Not something, Polly. Someone."

Polly nodded and kissed her mother's cool forehead as she turned to leave the room.

CHAPTER 33

After Florence left the room, it was Margaret Dye's turn to lie awake, staring into the darkness. How amazing to think God could use a diary from the past to answer her prayers for Florence in the present.

Sarah Davis. What had she written in those pages that had grabbed hold of her daughter's heart? The situation reminded her of something William Cowper had written: "God moves in mysterious ways, His wonders to perform."

Closing her eyes, Margaret drew a deep breath. "You do move in mysterious ways, Father. Help me trust you with my children. You know it's my desire for Florence's faith to be so strong that her relationship with you is the most important one in her life—so your influence over her is greater than mine."

Margaret pushed away the double wedding ring quilt her mother had given her and Robert as a wedding gift. She should have asked Florence to open a window. "I want her to have a relationship with you that is truly her own, not just an extension of my relationship with you. As the saying goes, *You have no grandchildren, only children*, Father."

Opening her eyes, Margaret stared upward again. "Lately, I've wanted an assurance that when my life is over, Florence's faith will be strong enough to uphold her, that she will know *you* are her strength. I want that for all my children, of course, but I especially want it for Florence."

Margaret turned over and felt a gentle kick from the baby in her womb. "Father, I don't know why this is happening to me. Maybe it's your way of reminding me to be still and know you are

God. There's so little I can do about most things except pray. You're in control."

Closing her eyes and taking slow deep breaths, Margaret tried to stop the flow of her prayers in hopes that she would fall asleep. Then she allowed her eyelids to drift open again. Prayers for her daughter were more important than sleeping.

"Thank you, Father, for sending Reverend Caldwell to our church last Christmas. Florence hasn't asked any pointed questions since that day about why you don't prevent pain and suffering. Whatever prompted her questions, I'm thankful she hasn't seemed so angry at you since then."

As she whispered these words, her breathing slowed. "I trust you, Lord, with my precious daughter, with all my precious children and my dear husband Bob. We've been so blessed."

Margaret slipped into peaceful slumber.

♠

The next day flew by as Polly ran the household—with a lot of help from her siblings. By the time Father and Ben returned from the mines for supper, Polly's feet and back ached. Ignoring the discomfort, she hummed a song from last Sunday's service as she fixed dinner with one hand and held Twila on her hip with the other.

Father entered the dining room waving a copy of The Evening Record under her nose. "What do you think I found in tonight's edition?" He raised an eyebrow at Polly.

So much had happened in the last few days, Polly hadn't any idea what her father meant. When she shook her head, he responded, "The outcome of Dr. Girard's trial."

How could she have forgotten? Mr. Boyd had mentioned day before yesterday that Kitt and her brother had gone to Atlantic City for the trial of the so-called "Dr." Girard.

Her father handed her the newspaper. "Page three." He held out his arms to Twila.

Polly turned the pages and read the headline. "Dr. Gerald, Kidnapper; Convicted."

"Dr. Gerald?" Polly glanced at her father. "I thought it was Dr. Girard."

Father shrugged. "I guess the newspapers misspelled his name."

"Fake Doctor Arrested at Atlantic City, Found Guilty After Highly Sensational Trial." Polly read the headline aloud. The location given was Mays Landing, NJ. Seeing Kitt's name in the newspaper again, Polly pitied her friend.

The last sentence of the article said, "Dr. Frank M. Gerald was tried and convicted on a technical charge after a hearing teeming with highly sensational evidence."

Looking at her father, Polly said, "That's it? What was the man's sentence?"

"I have no idea." Father frowned. "Maybe The Evening Record didn't get all the facts. Surely someone will have that information sooner or later."

"Do you know if Kitt is home yet?"

"Someone at the Post Office said they were coming home by train some time today." Father handed Twila back to Polly. "How's your mother doing?"

"She's doing very well. Beth has been a wonderful help, running up and down the stairs checking on her and taking her fruit and sandwiches. George and Robert got some weeding done."

Father sniffed as he went to wash and change his clothes. "Something smells good."

"Mrs. Patton brought us a chicken casserole and a couple of other neighbors brought us cookies and vegetables."

Finding Maggie in the sitting room reading to Elsie, Polly handed Twila to her sister. "Would you watch her, please, while I get supper on the table?"

Just then, Beth skipped down the stairs. Polly hugged her. "Could you set the table? You've been such a good helper today."

Beth beamed and headed for the kitchen. *Thank you, Father.* Polly hesitated. She was still shy about talking to God. *You truly have given us all grace and strength for this day.*

As she turned toward the kitchen, footsteps on the front porch steps drew her to the living room window. Kitt was walking toward the door. Polly hurried to open it. "You're back. How did things go?"

"It was awful." Kitt's eyes filled with tears. "They made me go through all the details again. One after another, the lawyers kept asking me questions and making me repeat things. I think the professor's lawyer was trying to mix me up."

"The Evening Record didn't give 'Dr. Gerald's' sentence."

"He got off too easy. Six months in the county jail in May's Landing and a fifty-dollar fine." Kitt's mouth twisted. "They said it was the maximum penalty that could be imposed." A tear slipped down her cheek.

"That's not right." Heat crept up Polly's neck and cheeks. "He'll be out in no time."

"I hated all this publicity but maybe it will keep people from being as gullible as I was."

Polly frowned. "I hope so. Would you like to stay for supper? Mother is on bed rest for two weeks, so I need to get our meal on the table."

Turning toward the door, Kitt shook her head. "Mother and Bess are making a special dinner for me to celebrate the trial being over. Is the baby okay?"

"We hope so. Dr. Cooley was afraid of labor beginning early. The baby isn't due until August."

Kitt nodded. "My sister, Bess, said Blanche Davis stopped in earlier today to see if we could help with meals, so she went to the market to buy a few things to fix some of our favorite recipes."

"Thanks, Kitt. Thanks for coming to tell us the news. I'll be praying for you."

The words slipped out of Polly's mouth and her eyebrows went up. It might have been the first time she'd told someone *she* would pray for them, rather than saying she'd ask her mother to pray.

"Thank you, Father," she whispered. "You are truly becoming real."

CHAPTER 34

Polly slumped on the sofa, her eyelids drooping, as Father read to Twila and Elsie. She rubbed the spot in her upper back that often ached, and flexed her weary feet. Though she worked hard every day, she'd had no idea how much of the household burden Mother carried.

Beth had just made another trip up the stairs, then sped back down. "Polly, Mother wants to talk to you."

Stifling a sigh, Polly got up and trudged toward the landing at the bottom of the stairs. She had promised Mother they'd talk later. Could she generate enough energy to walk up the steps? *One step at a time.* If only she had Beth's energy to run up and down all day.

As she reached the landing, there was a knock on the front door. She peered through the screen door and saw Garrett's suntanned face. Her pulse quickened. She hadn't even thought about him since Mother had been doing poorly and she'd started talking to God. *What does God think of my relationship with Garrett Young?*

Polly squared her shoulders. Right now her priority was seeing Mother, not going out with Garrett. Instead of inviting him in, she joined him on the porch where the fragrance of honeysuckle permeated the air.

"Hi Garrett."

"Hi." Garrett gave her a lazy grin. "Wanna go for a ride? I brought the buggy tonight because it's such a pleasant evening."

She hadn't been outside all day. A buggy ride would be heavenly. Polly set her jaw. "Maybe you haven't heard my mother isn't well. I have my hands full taking care of her, the children, and the house."

Garrett's eyes narrowed. "What seems to be her problem *this* time?"

He made it sound like her mother was a hypochondriac. "She's in the family way. The doctor's afraid the baby will come too soon, so she has to stay in bed."

The corners of Garrett's mouth turned down. "Can't someone else take care of her for a little while so you can go out with me?"

"Yes, they could. But Mother asked to see me just before you came. It might be important."

"Talking to her is more important than being with me?"

Polly looked him in the eye. "Yes."

He looked away and snorted. "As usual."

"If that's what you choose to believe, so be it." Polly turned to go back into the house and couldn't resist adding, "Since I haven't seen you for a couple of weeks, obviously you've had more important things than me, too."

Polly went inside, slamming the screen door behind her. There was approval in her father's eyes and peace in her heart as she headed for the stairs.

♠

Margaret wriggled herself upright on her pillows as Florence entered the bedroom. "Were you talking to someone on the porch?"

Florence's gaze darted to the open window. "I was talking to Garrett. He wanted me to go for a buggy ride. I told him talking with you is more important."

A lump rose in Margaret's throat. "Thank you, Florence."

"What did you want to talk about?" Florence moved closer to the bed.

"About that diary you read. You said the woman's name was Sarah Davis?"

"Yes."

"Why do you think you were supposed to read it?" Margaret leaned toward her daughter.

Florence reached behind her to pull a chair nearer, then sat down and took Mother's hand. "The day we moved into this house,

I had an apprehensive feeling when I walked through the door. I've had that same feeling on and off ever since..." She paused. "Especially in this room."

Priding herself on being a no-nonsense person, Margaret hated to admit she had wrestled with this feeling herself. But she had to be honest. "I've felt that way, too, at times."

Florence's mouth dropped. "Really? I was sure you'd say it was just my overactive imagination."

"You do have an active imagination, but this time I have to agree with you."

"When I found the diary, I thought maybe I'd discover that something bad had happened here before we moved in."

"Did you?"

"Eventually, but not through the diary. I *did* find out Sarah Davis was an amazing woman. She had a strong faith in God even though she and her husband, Thomas, had lost *five* daughters by the time they moved into this house."

"Five daughters. Is that what you were reading when you asked why God lets bad things happen to good people?"

"Yes." Florence balled her hands into fists. "I was so angry because I thought it was up to God to keep our lives free from pain."

Margaret searched her daughter's face. "And then?"

"And then Reverend Caldwell's sermon helped me understand why God sometimes allows us to experience pain."

"I thought so." Margaret nodded. "So the diary didn't explain why we sometimes have an ominous feeling in this house?"

"No, but it gave me a clue so I knew who to ask."

Margaret raised her eyebrows.

"The diary told me that Harry Davis, Blanche's husband, was the grandson of the original owners of this house. When she came to find out how you were doing last night, I asked her if something bad happened in this house."

Margaret choked and coughed. "You don't beat around the bush, do you?"

"A bad habit I know." Florence grimaced. "Words just come out of my mouth before I think. Blanche was shocked at my question. Then she told me what happened after Sarah died. Such awful things."

Florence told her mother about Nancy's mental illness, all the deaths, and then RV being declared a lunatic in this very room.

"Oh, my." Margaret closed her eyes. "We need to walk through every room and pray for the Holy Spirit to cleanse this place. We need to ask Him to close any doors that were opened to the enemy at that time."

Florence's eyes shone. "You always know what to do. I want to learn more about the Holy Spirit, but first let me tell you something else I learned about Sarah Davis."

Settling back into her pillows, Margaret gazed at her daughter. "What did you learn?"

Clasping her mother's hand, Florence told her how Sarah's diary ended, repeating the now-familiar words, "*Father, I have always put my trust in you. If only I had...*"

Her green eyes glowed. "Blanche said because of all Sarah's losses, she had become over protective of her children and encouraged them to depend on her, rather than depending on God."

Margaret took a deep breath, remembering her prayer of the night before. "So Blanche thought Sarah intended to say, *If only I had taught my children to put their trust in you.*"

Florence nodded, her auburn hair trembling. "Yes, that's it exactly. Blanche told me she survived *her* losses by learning from Sarah's mistakes, learning to put her trust in God. That's what got her through."

"So what did *you* learn from all this?"

"I learned I was way too much like Sarah's children. *You* have deep faith in God, but *I've* just had strong faith in you. All this time, I've thought of God as *Mother's God,* but last night that all changed." Florence clasped her hands over her heart. "I have my own relationship with God now. You've taught me so much, Mother. Now it's time to build on that foundation so I can be strong whatever happens."

Margaret's vision blurred and Florence touched her hand. "Why are you crying? Did I say something to upset you?"

"No, my darling daughter. These are tears of joy because God is answering my prayers in ways I could never have imagined. Who would ever have thought God would accomplish all this through an old diary?"

CHAPTER 35

Garrett mercilessly whipped the horses as he sped away from Polly's house. How dare she give him the brush off? *In a competition between her mother and me, I always lose.*

What about the times she did what you wanted when she knew her mother disapproved? Garrett scowled and brushed his hand across his eyes.

She was such a Mama's girl. Fine. Lots of other girls would love to spend time with him.

Allowing the horses to slow down, he debated what to do. Either the lovely blonde Delores Tribbley or the dark and mysterious Esther Tribbley would be a good companion for the evening, but if he went to their house, they might both be home.

Up until now, he'd been able to hide the fact that he was seeing them both, asking whichever one he saw in town to meet him somewhere. It was a risky game, but that was part of the appeal. He'd always asked them not to tell a soul.

He looked up. With the reins slack, the horses had headed for Jackson Center. Jackson Center. Where Savannah lived. Neither of the Tribbley girls, or any other girl for that matter, could compare to Savannah's violet blue eyes, lovely face, and stunning figure.

What about her character? Garrett wrinkled his forehead. He'd never worried about a girl's character before. If only Mr. Sullivan had never come to the store. What was it Savannah had said to him before they'd parted ways? *I'd hoped you might see things my way and agree that we are well suited for each other.*

"If she thought I'd agree we were well suited to each other, I guess that doesn't say much about my character either." Garrett wrinkled his forehead. "Maybe Savannah is right—maybe we *are* well suited to each other. Maybe we *do* want the same things in life."

Garrett's shoulders relaxed as he admitted there might be truth to what Savannah said. The tension of pretending he had higher morals than she did had worn him out. The truth was that if he was in her shoes and his parents didn't have the money to buy him the fancy things he craved, he'd probably do almost anything to get them.

At the outskirts of Jackson Center, he pulled on the reins, then guided the horses down a dirt road on his left where a little brook flowed through the trees.

Garrett leaped from the buggy, walked to the brook and sat on a large rock. What was it his mother often said to him about their wealth? *It's not because we deserve it that we have money and possessions; it's only by God's grace.* He could just as easily have been born into a family like Savannah's who had very little money, so who was he to judge her?

He that is without sin among you, let him cast the first stone. He turned to see who had spoken.

♠

Polly sat on the couch relishing the peacefulness of the house now that the younger children were in bed. The aroma of vegetable soup Kitt had brought for dinner still hung in the air. Father was upstairs spending time with Mother while Maggie and Ben had gone for a walk to enjoy the warm summer evening.

Mother's two weeks of bed rest were almost over. Dr. Cooley had said unless something else developed, she could be up for part of the day starting tomorrow. She needed to continue to rest often, however, and spend two to four hours a day lying down until the baby came.

"Thank you, Father," Polly whispered, "that Mother is doing well, and thank you for grace and strength for the rest of us during this difficult time."

Picking up her Bible engraved with her name, Polly flipped through the still-new pages. She'd gotten it for her 18th birthday but had never opened it except in church. If she wanted to have strong faith in God, it seemed appropriate for her to read her Bible. But where to begin? Someone had once recommended a beginner should start in the New Testament. Instead, she turned to the first chapter of the first book of the Bible. *In the beginning...*

In the beginning... What had it been like in the beginning, the beginning of time, the beginning of the world? The next word said it all, *In the beginning, God...*

When she was a little girl, Polly had asked her mother a question. "Mama, when was God born?" Her mother had stooped to her level. "God was never born. He has no beginning and He has no end. He has always been and He always will be."

Polly hadn't understood. She still didn't understand One who had always existed, but it was comforting to know that in the beginning, God was there.

She went on to the second verse. *...and the Spirit of God moved upon the face of the waters.* There it was again, that word. Spirit. Were the Spirit of God and the Holy Spirit the same? She had almost added, "thing," but Mother had corrected her when she'd referred to the Holy Spirit as "some thing."

Polly read the Genesis account of creation, including Adam and Eve and the perfect world they lived in. She still wanted a world like that. A world without pain, without fear, without death. Reverend Caldwell had said pain wasn't part of God's original plan.

Now the serpent was more subtle than any beast of the field which the Lord God had made. The perfect world hadn't remained perfect for long. Could she close the Bible and make believe she was in Eden before things went wrong?

But even in Eden, there was a serpent. With a sigh, Polly whispered something she'd heard her mother say. "For perfect, we have to wait for heaven, don't we, Father?"

When did I begin turning my thoughts into prayers, connecting with my heavenly Father wherever I am and whatever I'm doing? It was like the new connectedness she felt with her father since he'd come to her room the day she'd seen Garrett with his new love.

If my earthly father had treated me differently growing up, would I have come to know my Heavenly Father sooner? There was no way to know. Maybe if he'd been the perfect father, she wouldn't have discovered how much she needed her Heavenly Father.

She picked up her Bible. *And [the serpent] said to the woman...*

Chapter 36

A cool breeze swirled around Polly as she stepped onto the front porch. No sweat slid down her spine for a change. What a relief.

Hoof beats came down Broad Street as the Potter's buggy approached her, its top partially down.

"Good morning, Polly." Catherine Potter stopped the buggy under the shade tree in front of the house. "Do you think the heat wave's really over?"

"I'm afraid to hope. Father says it's the worst the northeast has ever had."

"Of all times for it to start—almost 100 degrees on the fourth of July. We didn't even go to the fireworks." Catherine settled her hat more securely on her head.

"Neither did we. Mother was just getting on her feet again." Polly sighed. "Father insisted she do as little as possible. We just tried to keep cool."

"Could you get any ice?"

"A little. It's so scarce and expensive, but Father wanted cool cloths around Mother's neck all the time." Polly leaned on the porch railing.

"Did you hear that more than 300 people died from the heat?" Catherine's eyebrows rose.

"Yes. Ever since Father told me I haven't sent the children out to work in the garden."

"What are they doing today?" Catherine's sleek black stallions flicked their tails against the flies that buzzed around them.

"With the cooler weather, Twila and Elsie finally settled down for a nap. Beth invited Robert and George to play jacks, and," Polly shrugged, "my best guess is Maggie's curled up somewhere with a book."

"Would you like to ride into Hadley with me? My friend Eunice's baby is due any day. Kitt didn't want to come."

Polly hesitated. "I'd love to go, but I'd better not. Father likes me to stay around when he's not home in case Mother has another spell. Right now she's lying down trying to satisfy her quota of hours of bed rest."

"Maybe next time." Catherine waved and clicked to the horses.

Polly went into the house and flopped on the couch in the sitting room with a sigh that rocked her whole body. Would this summer never end? *I've barely had time to breathe, Father, let alone think. Thank you for reminding me, as I read in Psalms today, that we are but dust. You don't expect more of us than we can give.*

Closing her eyes, she rested in the knowledge of God's grace. She wanted to sleep but instead a still small voice whispered a question she'd been avoiding. *What does God think of your relationship with Garrett Young?*

That question again. Did God agree with her parents' estimation of Garrett? If she were honest, she'd have to admit she spent a lot of time making excuses to herself and her parents for his behavior. Why did she feel it necessary to do that?

Time to stop making excuses for Garrett's behavior—the little things, as well as the big ones. Polly wrinkled her forehead, let out another body-rocking sigh, then set her lips in a straight line.

A light tap on the front door interrupted her. She jumped up and rushed to greet the visitor before louder knocks wakened the girls. Kitt stood there with her shoulder-length dark hair skinned back from her forehead and pulled into a tight bun, a prim, dark green dress with long sleeves buttoned up to her chin. She could have passed for a spinster school marm.

"Kitt. How are you doing? I just saw your mother. Would you like to come in?" Plenty of time later to examine her relationship with Garrett.

"I just wanted to ask about your mother's health."

"She's still on partial bed rest but feeling much better."

Kitt peered past Polly into the living room. "Do you have time to visit?"

"Sure." Polly opened the door wider. "Everyone else is either sleeping, reading or playing a game."

She led Kitt into Mother's sitting room. "You look... different."

"Trying to stay as far away from men as I can. They're not to be trusted, you know." Kitt pushed her hairpins deeper into her bun.

"In spite of the bad experience you had, I don't think that's true of *all* men." Polly bit her lip. "But I agree we have to be careful who we trust. Actually, I've been thinking about my relationship with Garrett."

"I'm glad to hear that."

"You've never liked Garrett much have you?"

Kitt wrinkled her nose. "No, but you're always making excuses for him."

Polly giggled. "I think you're reading my mind. I had just reached that conclusion myself."

"So, is it time to stop making excuses for the things he does that upset you?"

Closing her eyes, Polly nodded.

"Wanna talk about it?"

"Probably a good idea. Maybe it'll help if I have an audience to keep me honest." She held up one finger. "First of all, he's lazy and unreliable. For example, he didn't get up in time to come and help my family load our furniture when we moved, and he was always finding excuses not to go to work at the mill. Plus, he can't be bothered to walk to my front door when we go out."

Kitt was vigorously nodding her head when Polly opened her eyes. Tugging the cushion into a more comfortable position behind her, Polly frowned and screwed up her forehead. She preferred to focus on people's positive qualities, but in Garrett's case, this had amounted to sheer blindness.

Eyes glowing, Kitt touched her arm. "What else?"

Kitt probably loved this because it seemed to confirm her opinion of men after her experience with the fake doctor. "Maybe this wasn't such a good idea—"

"Didn't you say he criticizes your mother a lot?"

Polly swallowed hard. "He criticizes her *all* the time. He loves to imply she's a hypochondriac or lazy, neither of which is true."

"That's not good. If you get married, you'd be caught in the middle, trying to keep peace between them." Kitt sat up straight. "Don't you think?"

Getting up to pace the tiny room, Polly counted her steps under her breath. "One, two, three, four," turn, "One, two, three, four," turn...

"Polly? I know it can be hard to be honest with yourself, but I wasn't honest with myself about Dr. Gerard and look where it got me."

Stomping her foot, Polly turned toward Kitt. "You're right. I *know* you're right. I *hate* being wrong. I need to be honest with myself but the hardest thing to admit is that Garrett isn't honest—period. I can never prove it though, because he has a way with words that confuses me. My parents taught me that truth is important, but I suspect he doesn't agree."

"How do you think his dishonesty will affect his relationship with his future wife?" Kitt had moved to the edge of the couch.

"My parents' relationship is built on mutual trust." Polly paused. "My mother never worries that my father might be lying to her, nor does my father worry about my mother telling him lies."

Kitt looked straight into Polly's eyes. "Have you thought about what it would be like to live with somebody you didn't trust? I did that in Atlantic City for a month. It was a nightmare."

Polly wilted and plopped on the floor. "I'm sure you're right again. I thought I loved Garrett, but besides everything else, he isn't willing to make a commitment or even say he loves me. Sometimes he compliments me but..." She couldn't tell Kitt she suspected his compliments were to win her heart so she would allow him the liberties he wanted without any commitment.

"...but you think he's complimenting you so you'll allow him to take advantage of you." Kitt dropped down beside Polly on the floor.

Polly's eyes widened. Then she straightened her shoulders. "Exactly."

"I'm glad you're starting to tell yourself the truth about Garrett." Kitt patted Polly's arm.

"Even more important, I know my Heavenly Father approves." Polly smiled.

Raising her eyebrows, Kitt stood up. "I'd better get home now. Bess will be wondering where I am."

As Kitt descended the steps to the street, Polly gripped the railing and prayed softly, "I don't know why I've been so stubborn about my relationship with Garrett, Father. Maybe it's partly because I hate admitting my parents were right about him."

When the Spirit of truth comes, He will guide you into all truth. She must have memorized that verse as a child.

"Spirit of truth," she murmured. "Probably another name for the Spirit of God and the Holy Spirit. When I was ready to listen, did the Spirit of truth come to show me the truth about Garrett?"

♠

As Polly wiped the last dish from dinner, the crunching of tires on the hard-packed dirt road in front of their house drew her. Dr. Cooley and Garrett were the only people who came to the Dye residence in a car, and Polly knew they weren't expecting Dr. Cooley. The rest of the family had scattered after supper with Maggie taking charge of the little ones, so Polly walked to the screen door.

"Hi Polly." Garrett's voice was low. "Could you come with me for a walk?"

Polly hesitated. What should she do? She regretted she'd led Garrett on because she was bored. Perhaps taking a walk would be the best way to tell him she couldn't see him anymore.

Pressing through her sadness at what she must do, Polly swallowed the lump in her throat. She opened the screen door and stepped out on the porch where the evening breeze swirled her skirts. "Yes, we can walk. I need to talk to you."

"I need to talk to you, too."

She stole a few glances at him. Something was different.

Together they walked down the front porch steps and onto the road. Then they spoke at the same time. "What did you want to talk about?"

Smiling, Garrett said, "Ladies first."

She sent up a silent prayer. *What should I say, Lord?* She took a deep breath. "We've had a lot of fun together."

"Yes, we have."

"But I don't think we should see each other any more. Mother will be having her baby soon—" Polly stopped. "That isn't the real reason. I have to be honest with you."

Keeping his eyes on the road, Garrett nodded and waited.

"I've been doing a lot of thinking and... and praying lately, asking myself what God thinks of our relationship. I haven't been completely honest with you, Garrett, and I don't think you've been honest with me."

Swallowing hard, Polly stopped in the middle of the road. "I... I... I don't see the qualities and character traits in you that... that I want in the man I marry." She gulped. "I know you've said you're not ready to get married, but I believe dating should include building a foundation for marriage."

Gently, Garrett cupped Polly's elbow and guided her off the road and down a trail that led to the creek. Then he turned and looked into her eyes. "I asked you to come on this walk because I owe you an apology. I've been doing a lot of thinking, and yes, even praying, too."

Polly could hardly keep her mouth from hanging open.

Garrett plowed on. "I *haven't* been honest with you. I've toyed with your feelings. Even though I told you we'd get married some day, I was using you as one more woman to have on my string."

Eyes widening. Polly's brows inched toward her hairline with each word Garrett spoke.

"Can you forgive me?" Garrett's forehead wrinkled over his pleading blue eyes.

Taking a step back, Polly frowned. Was this just another ploy to keep her from walking away from him?

"I don't blame you for not trusting me." Garrett cleared his throat. "I haven't given you any reason to trust me. I just want to make things right before I move on."

Move on? This wasn't going the way Polly had expected. "Are you saying you don't want to continue seeing me?"

"You're a wonderful girl, Polly, and I don't want to hurt you more than I already have. The truth is, I'm in love with someone else."

Pasting a smile on her face, Polly took a deep breath. Garrett must never know she'd hoped he'd try to change her mind. She hadn't known it herself. "I'll forgive you, Garrett, if you'll forgive me. I hope you and the girl you love will be very happy."

CHAPTER 37

As Garrett's car pulled away from the front of the house, Polly restrained her first impulse to run to Mother's bedroom where she had gone to rest after supper. Instead, she marched up the stairs into her own bedroom and closed the door. Kneeling beside her bed, Polly buried her face in the patchwork quilt her mother had pieced and quilted with the women from their church.

"Father," she wept, but no other words came. With deep sobs that shook her whole body, she reached for her Bible on the oak bedside table. Blindly, Polly opened it at random, looking for something, anything to comfort her. Her sobbing stilled as she read verse 26 of the eighth book of Romans. *Likewise the Spirit also helpeth our infirmities: for we know not what we should pray for as we ought: but the Spirit Himself maketh intercession for us with groanings which cannot be uttered.*

"Holy Spirit—" Polly hesitated. Was it okay to pray to the Holy Spirit? She would ask Mother but it felt right. "I am so weak right now. I know Garrett isn't the right man for me, but rejection hurts so much. Please help me in my weakness—give me strength to get through this."

She pulled a clean hanky from her pocket and blew her nose. "I'm so thankful you're praying for me with groanings that cannot be uttered. I know Mother prays for me and probably Father too, but I never knew you prayed for me, Holy Spirit. If you're groaning, maybe that means you're also feeling my pain."

There was a light tap on the door, and Beth's sweet voice called, "Polly, are you in there? Can I come in?"

Polly wiped her eyes, only Beth would have knocked. The boys and probably even Maggie would have barged right in.

"Come in, Beth."

Beth pushed open the door and poked her head around it. She started to say something, and then stopped and walked over to the bed. "Are you okay?" She patted Polly's cheek,

"I will be, Honey. What do you need?"

"I checked on Mother and she asked if you have time to talk."

"Of course. Tell her I'll be right there. I need to run downstairs for a minute."

Taking the steps two at a time, Polly sprinted to the kitchen for water to wash her face. She didn't want Mother to know she'd been crying. What did she want to talk about? She could hardly wait to tell her what she'd been learning about the Holy Spirit.

♠

"Pull up a chair and sit down, Florence." Margaret smiled at her oldest daughter and relaxed among her pillows. Why were her eyes red? Florence didn't cry often and not without good reason. "What's wrong, dear?"

Florence sighed. "I didn't want you to know I'd been crying."

"Why?"

"Because I need to learn to go to God with my problems, not just run to you."

"And did you go to God with this problem?" Margaret reached for Florence's hand.

"Yes, yes I did. At first, I didn't know what to say. But when I opened the Bible, I found a verse about the Spirit helping us in our weaknesses and praying for us. I didn't know the Holy Spirit prays for us."

"He does many things people don't know He does."

"I still have lots of questions about the Holy Spirit although God has been teaching me. Spirit of God, Spirit of truth, and Holy Spirit...are those all names for the same thing—I mean person?"

"Yes, dear, they're all the same—all names for the third person of the Trinity."

"I've heard about the Trinity, about God the Father and Jesus, God's Son, and the Holy Spirit. But how come no one ever talks much about the Holy Spirit?"

"Maybe because most people don't understand Him, even though He is so important. He comes to live in our hearts when we repent of our sins and receive Jesus."

"I didn't know that."

"The Holy Spirit is often like a person who comes to live in someone's house but is never received, made welcome, because the people in the house aren't aware of His presence." Margaret smiled at her lovely daughter. "What else has God been teaching you about the Holy Spirit?"

"Well, like today, a still small voice asked me what God thought of my relationship with Garrett. Then Kitt came by and encouraged me to talk about his poor character traits I've been excusing. I believe the Holy Spirit used that conversation to show me the truth about Garrett. Mother, do you think maybe I'm learning to be guided by Him rather than following my own desires and schemes?"

Tears came to Margaret's eyes as her daughter expressed spiritual truths she had so longed for Florence to understand. *Thank you, Holy Spirit, for guiding her to the truth.*

"I believe you are, dear. Did I hear Garrett's car earlier?"

Florence bit her lip and nodded.

"Did you talk to him about what the Holy Spirit showed you?"

With tears slipping down her cheeks, Florence relayed her conversation with Garrett. "I really think he's changed, Mother, but—" She gulped and took a deep breath.

Margaret squeezed her daughter's hand.

"He says he's in love with someone else."

"Oh, Little One." Margaret wiped Florence's eyes on the corner of the sheet.

"Even though I didn't plan to keep seeing him, it hurt so much when he told me."

Margaret reached out and pulled Florence close. Her own heart ached. "Do you know another name for the Holy Spirit, Little One? Jesus sometimes called Him the Comforter."

"Really?" Florence's eyes widened.

"Really. I'm praying the Comforter will come and heal your broken heart."

"Thank you, Mother." Florence paused and closed her eyes. "Do you remember when Reverend Caldwell asked if we dared to believe that sometimes pain is God's good gift to us? That pain produces qualities we wouldn't develop any other way?"

"I remember."

"Is that why He's allowing this to happen to me?"

"Perhaps. The Bible says God comforts us in our trials so we'll be able to comfort others when they need comfort. It says our Heavenly Father is the God of all comfort."

"Oh, Mama, that is so beautiful! I need to write it down."

Margaret smiled fondly as her high-spirited daughter, in despair only a moment before, dashed from the room to get writing supplies.

A dark cloud passed over the sun that had been beaming in Margaret's window. Times of intense learning were often followed by times of intense testing. *Was Florence being prepared for a test?*

CHAPTER 38

The knock on Savannah's door was loud and demanding. She hurried to answer it with a ripple of fear. Her landlord and tavern owner, Mr. Burns, stood outside with a scowl on his swarthy face. The smell of unwashed flesh was strong. When Savannah moved in, he had agreed to let her conduct business here if she gave him a percentage of her earnings, but this looked like trouble.

"Sheriff DeLancy says if you don't stop what you're doing, he'll arrest me for keeping a bawdy house. When I told him I didn't know nothin' about you doing such things, he said people are willin' to testify against you and me."

Savannah couldn't breathe. "But Mr. Burns, you promised..."

"I didn't promise you nothin', and ya can't prove otherwise. I run an honest business here. I can't have the likes of you messin' things up for me."

"Can I at least keep living here?"

Mr. Burns opened and closed his fists. "I'll give ya two weeks to find another place, but absolutely no visitors. Ya hear me?"

Savannah nodded as her landlord stomped down the stairs. She closed the door but couldn't move. What would she do? She'd always depended on her good looks to get what she needed and wanted.

Wrinkling her forehead, she slumped on the edge of the bed. Who would be willing to help her? When women passed her on the street, they either crossed to the other side or pulled their skirts close to them, as though brushing hers might contaminate them. Because of the nature of her business, even her clients kept clear if they saw her in town.

Standing up, Savannah went and gazed out the window. People walking up and down the wooden sidewalks looked like they had some place to go. She couldn't go back to Georgia even if she wanted to. Her family would have nothing to do with her. They'd washed their hands of her when they found out what she'd become. Her mother told her in a letter, "We may be poor, but at least we earn our money honestly. You've brought disgrace and shame upon your family and upon God."

She began to pace from door to window in the tiny, stuffy room. God. It was likely He had washed His hands of her too. He probably tilted His nose in the air just like the town's people when He looked at sinners like her. Ma had taught her right from wrong, but she'd made up her mind as a teenager she wasn't going to live in poverty no matter what she had to do to avoid it. She hadn't asked for God's help so she certainly couldn't turn to Him now.

Footsteps came up the stairs and approached her door. What if it was one of her clients? Mr. Burns would throw her out on the spot. The knock on her door was firm but not intimidating as Mr. Burns' knock had been.

Holding her breath, she opened the door a crack. Her pulse quickened. It was Garrett.

He smiled and put his hand on the doorknob. "The lady downstairs told me I'd find you here."

"You can't come in." Savannah started to close the door in Garrett's face, but he was too quick, sliding his foot in the opening.

"Then come with me for a ride. Please?" Savannah hesitated. Garrett stretched out his hand. "It's really a nice day now that the heat wave is over."

Savannah stepped out in the hall, pulling the door closed behind her. "Okay, but when we come back, you can't come to my room."

"I wasn't planning to come to your room. What's wrong?"

"We can't talk here." Savannah started down the stairs with Garrett close behind her. As she hurried across the dining room, Mr. Burns' glare was enough to take her breath.

Almost blinded by the bright sunshine outside, she allowed Garrett to open the car door for her. He cranked the car until it roared to life and then drove down the street.

Hands clenched in her lap, she stared out the window waiting for Garrett to ask questions she wouldn't want to answer. What could he possibly want? She gritted her teeth as he turned down a little dirt road.

"There's a nice creek a little ways from here." Garrett smiled at Savannah. "I have a blanket we can sit on while we talk."

Still saying nothing, Savannah got out of the car, waited while he retrieved the blanket, and then followed him to the creek.

After spreading the blanket on the ground, Garrett reached for Savannah's hand. "Will you sit with me or are you still angry?"

Reluctantly, Savannah sat down as he lowered himself to the ground. "I'm not angry with you. I guess you could say I'm in trouble."

♠

At Savannah's words, everything Garrett had planned to say fled. "What kind of trouble?"

"My landlord says I have to get out or they're going to arrest him."

"I see." Garrett remembered Mr. Sullivan's words. *It's only a matter of time.* "What are you going to do?"

"I don't know. He told me just before you arrived." Savannah wrapped her arms around herself.

Garrett's forehead puckered. He didn't want Savannah to leave but he knew he should ask. "Could you go home to your parents?"

"They want nothing to do with me. I've brought shame and disgrace on them. Even God has washed His hands of me."

Sitting up straighter, Garrett looked into Savannah's eyes. "I don't believe that's true. Do you remember last time we talked, you told me you thought we were well-suited to each other? I was so angry, but you were right."

Savannah's eyes widened. "I was?"

Garrett nodded. "Even though I condemned you for what you were doing, I might have done the same thing in your shoes. My morals aren't any better than yours—only my circumstances are different. God showed me I'm no better than you."

"Then what makes you think God hasn't washed His hands of me?" Savannah plucked a thread from her dress.

"Because He's forgiven me for the things I've done and for my bad morals. I've apologized to some people I've hurt and made some things right. God's given me a new beginning. I can hardly believe the way He's changing me. He'll do the same for you if you want Him to." Garrett reached for Savannah's hand.

"But you haven't done the things I've done, even though you say you *might* have in my shoes."

"Last Sunday our pastor talked about a woman who'd been married five times. She was caught committing adultery. The church leaders wanted to stone her as the law of Moses commanded but when they brought the woman to Jesus, He didn't condemn her." He squeezed Savannah's hand. "Instead, He told her to go and sin no more. So if He forgave her, I believe He'd forgive you."

"But..."

"But what?" Garrett searched her eyes.

"I made a vow a long time ago I'd never ask God or anyone else for help. How can I ask Him now that I've made such a mess of my life?"

"The only thing stopping you is your pride, Savannah. That's what was stopping me. But now, I've even been reading the Bible and going to church with my mother. It finally became real to me what Jesus did." Garrett tilted Savannah's chin so her eyes met his. "Jesus died for every sin we've committed to make a way for us to have a relationship with God. But it won't do us any good if we're too proud to receive it."

Savannah closed her beautiful eyes and let her head drop toward her chest. His hand fell away. After a moment, she looked at him. "What are you doing here, Garrett? Why did you come?"

Garrett's voice was husky when he finally spoke. "Because, Savannah, I think I'm in love with you."

CHAPTER 39

Garrett climbed out of bed, yawning and rubbing his eyes. He had set his alarm a half hour earlier than usual because he needed to talk to his mother. First, he had some apologizing to do and then... he needed to talk to her about Savannah. How would she react? He shuddered. She had nearly always taken his side regardless of the situation, but this time he was afraid she'd think he'd gone too far.

He had told Savannah he'd try to work out a way for her to live in Sandy Lake. Without his parents' help, however, he couldn't do that. *Is this the right thing for me to do, Lord?*

Staring at his reflection in the mirror, Garrett shook his head. If anyone had told him a few weeks ago that he would be trying to help Savannah make a new beginning, he wouldn't have believed them. "Me," he mumbled, "Mr. Selfish, Mr. Look Out For Myself. It must be true what our preacher said last week from Paul's teachings, we *can* be new creatures in Christ. Nothing else makes any sense."

As he ran down the stairs, the smell of bacon frying wafted up to him. His mother stood by the stove frying eggs and bacon, cheeks rosy from the heat. He stepped toward her to kiss her cheek, but stopped. He always did that when he wanted something from her. So instead, he said, "Good morning, Ma. How'd you sleep?"

His mother peered at him, a puzzled frown on her face. She'd looked that way a lot since God started changing him. "I slept well, son. How about you?"

Garrett shook his head. "Got a lot on my mind."

"Oh? Trouble at work?"

"No, work's fine." He pulled a plate and glass from the shelf.

"Sorry breakfast isn't quite ready, son."

"Not your fault, Ma. I'm up early this morning. Have you eaten? Shall I get a plate for you?"

"That would be nice. Thank you."

In a few minutes, they sat across the table from each other with well-filled, fragrant plates. They bowed their heads, and his mother said a short prayer of thanks. Then she looked at her son. "If it isn't work, what's troubling you?"

Garrett swallowed hard, took a sip of juice and almost choked on the nervous words on his lips. He'd lain awake half the night trying to decide where to begin. His silver tongue that had always worked well seemed to be stumbling lately. His mother watched him with her forehead puckered again.

"Ma, you remember Savannah, the girl you met a couple months ago?"

"I remember. Why didn't you ever bring her back?"

"I stopped seeing her because I heard some bad rumors about her."

His mother put down her fork. "Maybe the rumors weren't true."

How like his mother to believe the best of people. "Oh, they were true, all right. She admitted it."

Her eyes widened. "What had she done?"

"Well, she... That is, her parents were very poor so she came here from Georgia to better herself. Life didn't work out the way she'd hoped and..." Garrett pushed back his plate, his food untouched, his stomach churning. "I'm sorry, Ma, I can't tell you what Savannah was doing. All I can say is I'd have made the same decisions as she if you and Pa weren't able to give me nice things."

As he returned his mother's steady gaze, Garrett thought her warm blue eyes had a hint of moisture in them.

"Where is Savannah now?"

"She's in Jackson Center. She has to move out of her room in two weeks and has nowhere to go. Her family wants nothing to do with her."

Mother nodded. "All right. Why don't you bring her home with you after work today, and I'll talk to her. I've always wanted a daughter. Maybe this is my chance to make a difference in this young woman's life."

Throwing his arms around her neck, Garrett said, "You're the best mother a fellow could ever have. Will you pray for me to be a better son?"

"I will, but I haven't always been the best mother either. I yearned for a baby, and we waited so long before God gave you to us. I indulged you and let you have your way far too often. Your father told me I'd ruin your character, but I didn't listen. I thought the more we did for you, the more you'd love us."

Garrett sat back down. "We both have some changes to make, don't we? But like our pastor said on Sunday, anything is possible with God."

"So you *were* listening. And here I thought you were just going to church because you wanted something from me."

"Not this time, Ma. I finally faced the truth about myself a few weeks ago. It was painful. That's when I started asking God to change me. Going to church seemed like a good place to start."

"You don't know how I've waited and prayed for this day, Garrett."

He rose from the table, bent over and kissed his mother's cheek. "I'd better go or I'll be late for work. Thanks so much for saying you'll talk to Savannah."

♠

Polly tiptoed into her parents' bedroom after she was sure Twila and Elsie were sleeping. Mother had asked her to return once she'd gotten the girls down for their nap. *Screech.* The board where Sarah's diary had been hidden creaked loudly as she stepped on it, and the same chill seized her that had crept up her spine the first time she'd done so.

Resting against her pillows, Mother shuddered at the noise.

"What did you want, Mother?"

"Interesting that you should step on that board just now. After we talked this morning, I remembered we'd never prayed through the house, asking the Holy Spirit to cleanse it of anything ungodly that may have entered during those tragic days when Sarah's family fell apart."

Glancing around the room, Polly nodded. "Since I talked to Blanche Davis about what happened here, I haven't had this eerie sensation until now. I hoped whatever was causing it had left, but maybe it was just hiding."

Mother swung her legs over the side of the bed and started putting on her shoes. "Let's do our praying while the little ones are sleeping and the other children are working in the garden. Maggie's supervising them."

Her mother picked up a little vial from her bedside table that Polly hadn't seen before. "What's that?"

"Anointing oil. Last Sunday I asked Reverend Lawrence for a little from the container he keeps on the communion table. There's nothing magical about it. It's symbolic of the Holy Spirit."

Together Polly and Mother walked down the stairs. Mother led the way to the front door. Putting a small amount of oil on her fingertip, she made the sign of the cross on the doorframe.

"Heavenly Father, thank you for providing this home for us. We know the original owners went through very hard times here, and since we've moved in, we've sensed something that is not of you. It's not important that we know exactly what's causing this, but we ask in Jesus' name that you'd cleanse our home and fill it with your Holy Spirit. Walk with us through our home, as we pray for the cleansing and filling of every room."

Mother held the vial out to her daughter. "Do you want to anoint the sitting room door frame and pray over that room?"

Polly shrank back. "I wouldn't know what to say."

"It doesn't have to be perfect, dear."

"I know. I know. *For perfect, we have to wait for heaven...*" Polly smiled and took the small bottle from her mother.

"It's only important to know the power to cleanse this house comes from the Holy Spirit, not from you."

They bowed their heads. Polly's mouth went dry and her heart fluttered in her chest. She hadn't prayed aloud with Mother since she'd started saying her own bedtime prayers. "Father, please cleanse this room and fill it with your Holy Spirit. Amen."

Taking turns anointing and praying, they made their way through all the rooms in the house, ending in her parents' room.

Mother took the anointing oil and anointed the doorframe and both window frames. "Father, we know this room belonged to the last member of the original family, when he was declared a lunatic. We don't know if it was a sanctuary or a prison to Vance, but it's here we've had the strongest sense of a dark presence. So we're asking you to cleanse this room of hopelessness, fear, and despair—anything that's not of you. Fill it with your hope, your peace, and your joy, regardless of the circumstances."

Pausing for a moment, Mother looked around the room. "We pray any doors that were opened to the enemy of our souls would be closed in Jesus' name and no evil presence would be allowed to remain. Our hope is in the Lord who made the heavens and the earth, and nothing is too difficult for you. Fill this room with your presence."

Polly had never experienced anything as powerful as Mother's prayer. It raised goose bumps on her arms even as it filled her with peace. She didn't want to open her eyes and she didn't want to move. "Hopelessness, fear, and despair. That's what we were sensing here, wasn't it? How did you know what to pray?"

"As I prayed, the Holy Spirit gave me wisdom and discernment. After He showed me, it made perfect sense."

"Will I ever be able to receive wisdom like that from the Holy Spirit?"

"If you live your life in tune with God's Spirit, His wisdom will become more and more available to you. If you live your life in tune with the world, then worldly wisdom will be yours. The choice will be up to you."

CHAPTER 40

With a little of his old swagger and flourish, Garrett Young opened the car door for Savannah. "Your chariot awaits, my lady."

Savannah didn't smile. "Why does your mother want to talk to me?" Her violet blue eyes were dark and her lips pursed.

Garrett ran around and jumped into the driver's seat and let out the clutch. "I told her you had to move out of your room in two weeks and had nowhere to go."

"Does she know why I have to move?"

"Not exactly. She knows I'd heard rumors about you which turned out to be true." Garrett made the turn onto the road to Sandy Lake.

"I don't know, Garrett. Maybe you should take me back. I don't see how talking to your mother is going to change anything."

"My mother said she'd always wanted a daughter and maybe this was her opportunity to make a difference in your life. You'll like my mother. She's wonderful."

Savannah lapsed into silence, her face turned away. Garrett could only guess at what she was thinking. He understood her fear of talking to his mother, but what other options did she have?

He glanced at Savannah. "Do you have any money saved?'

"What?" Savannah tilted her head in his direction. "Money saved? A little. Why?"

"You might be able to rent a room at the Cottage Hotel in Sandy Lake."

"They'll want references. And besides, without a job, the money won't last long." Savannah twisted and untwisted her long, slender fingers.

"With my mother's help, we might be able to bypass the references and find someone willing to hire you. My father says no one can say no to Ma." He winked at Savannah.

When she didn't respond, he sighed and sent up a silent prayer to the One who cared even more about Savannah's well-being than he did. *Please soften her heart, Father, and make her willing to accept the help she needs—from you and from me. Help her see there's a better way than the way she's been living. Help her learn to trust again.*"

♠

Savannah stared out the window as they sped toward Sandy Lake. She didn't bother looking at the scenery. What did it matter? More shame and condemnation probably awaited her at Garrett's house.

"You take after your father's side of the family," her mother used to say. "None of them were any good. I don't know what I was thinking, marrying into that family. 'Poor white trash,' is what my father called them, and he was right."

Even though Garrett's mother wouldn't know whose side of the family Savannah took after, she'd surely know after one glance that Savannah came from 'poor white trash.' Her mother had told her no matter what kind of fancy clothes she wore, people would *always* be able to tell.

Smoothing her satiny skirt between her fingers, Savannah stared at Garrett. Why was he doing this? He'd be in for a good tongue-lashing, and probably worse, when his parents found out what she'd been doing in Jackson Center. They'd surely think the worst about her relationship with him. Garrett had never visited her room, had never been one of her customers. Would they believe her?

My child, lift up your head, your redemption draws near. Where had she heard those words? Maybe in her grandma's little white church? Peace and hope settled around her. Perhaps there would be something Garrett's mother could do.

♠

As usual, Mildred Young heard her son's Model T before she saw it gliding into the driveway. She took off her apron and smoothed her hair. As she opened the door, Garrett ran around to the passenger's side of the car. Good manners had never been Garrett's way. Maybe the Lord *was* changing his heart.

Savannah got out of the car and Garrett turned toward Mildred. "Ma, you remember Savannah?"

Starting across the yard, Savannah's gaze flitted toward the house, the yard and everywhere except at Mildred.

"Of course I do. Hello Savannah." Mildred smiled, taking a few steps toward the edge of the porch.

When Savannah finally looked up and their eyes met, Mildred's pulse quickened. It wasn't Savannah's beauty that moved her. Something deeper. Underneath the lovely, well-put-together exterior, hid a lonely waif who desperately needed a mother.

As Savannah came up the porch steps, Mildred opened her arms and gathered her close. Behind her, Garrett's eyes lit up. Mildred smiled at him. "Why don't you give Savannah and me some time alone? Your father will be late tonight, so dinner won't be until around 7:00."

"All right with you, Savannah?"

He saw a tear trickling down her cheek as she nodded.

"Okay, Ma. I'll be back, Savannah."

♠

Garrett ambled aimlessly through town, eventually ending up on Broad Street. Polly and Kitt were coming toward him, talking in low tones.

"Hello, Ladies." Garrett tipped an imaginary hat.

"Hi, Garrett," they said in unison. Polly added, "Where are you going? I don't often see you out walking since you got your car."

"My mother wanted some time alone with a guest, so I'm making myself scarce. How's everyone at your house, Polly?"

Polly's eyes widened. Had he ever asked about her family before?

"We're doing okay. Mother is due any day now, so the doctor is pretty happy. He thinks the danger is past."

"How about you, Kitt? How are you doing?"

Kitt's eyebrows shot up. Her surprise was deserved since he'd never bothered to talk to her before. Probably because at some point, he'd decided she was a stuck up, rich kid.

She dropped her gaze and stared at her hands clasped in front of her. "You and the whole world know how stupid I am." Then her eyelids lifted, her dark eyes flashing. "But let it be said here and now I'll never trust another man. If Polly's smart, she won't either."

Heat rose in Garrett's cheeks, and he opened his mouth, then closed it, recognizing the familiar stirrings of his temper. He took a deep breath. "I don't blame you, Kitt, after all you've been through." He swallowed hard. "I haven't been trustworthy in the past, but I'm working on changing that."

Kitt grabbed Polly's arm. "Don't let him convince you, Polly. You'll be sorry."

"Garrett isn't interested in me, Kitt. I told you that." Polly patted her friend's hand. "Don't take it personally, Garrett. It's going to take some time for Kitt to get over—you know."

Garret nodded as Polly took Kitt's arm and turned her in the other direction. "Let's head back toward the creek."

♠

Garrett trudged past the stores on Main Street and up the hill toward Jackson Center, still smarting from Kitt's words. Not everyone was going to believe he'd changed without a lot of proof. *Father, help me be patient with people I've hurt. I can't expect them to believe me just because I* say *I've changed.*

He'd lost all track of time. Had he allowed Mother and Savannah enough time to talk? He turned and jogged toward home. As soon as he opened the door, Savannah came toward him, eyes sparkling. "You were right, Garrett. Your mother is wonderful. She talked with me and prayed with me. I'm done with my old life. God has forgiven me, and I'm working on forgiving myself."

Garrett squeezed Savannah's hand, and sprinted into the kitchen where he hugged his mother for a long time. Why had it taken him so long to see how blessed he was? How could he have been so blind?

CHAPTER 41

As Polly and Kitt walked toward the creek, Polly's parents strolled toward them arm in arm.

"I'm surprised to see Mother out and about. She can barely waddle these days." Polly raised her voice and called to her parents. "Where are you going?"

"It's such a beautiful evening, we wanted to enjoy the lovely weather. Maggie's watching the little ones." Mother smiled.

"You're feeling up to this?" Polly eyed her mother's bulging abdomen skeptically.

"As long as she doesn't overdo, Dr. Cooley said exercise is good for her." Father patted the hand tucked into the crook of his arm.

"If you're sure. I'd hate to see my little brother or sister being born somewhere along Broad Street." Polly grinned.

Her parents chuckled and continued down the street at a sedate pace.

Kitt sighed. "You're so lucky to have both parents, Polly. I miss my father and brothers so much. I still can't believe they're gone."

"I'm sorry, Kitt." Polly put her arm around her friend as they turned toward the creek. "I'll ask God to send the Holy Spirit to comfort you and your family. Mother says another name for the Holy Spirit is the Comforter."

Raising an eyebrow at Polly, Kitt shook her head. "I don't know about all this God stuff from you lately. Where was God when Mr. Gerard was deceiving me?"

"Your mother told you if the man was legitimate, he wouldn't have asked you not to tell her about him. You wouldn't tell me either. Maybe God was trying to stop you."

"Maybe." Kitt stared at the rippling water and then up into the oak trees that shaded them. "He should have tried harder."

Polly plopped down on the mossy ground and stared into the brook. "Did I tell you I found the diary of Sarah Davis, one of the original owners of our house?"

Kitt shook her head.

"They had lost five children by the time they moved to our house." Polly picked a few stones out of the clear water. "After she lost her first child, she wrote in her diary, *If I turn against God, to whom will I go for the comfort and strength I need to get through the days ahead?* No matter what happened, she never turned against God."

Dropping down beside her, Kitt started taking off her shoes. "What good did it do her? What good is God if He doesn't keep us from having trouble?"

"I understand how you feel because I felt the same way until Reverend Caldwell preached at our church last year."

Sock in hand, Kitt frowned. "What did he say?"

"He said sometimes pain and trouble are God's good gifts to produce the qualities we wouldn't develop in any other way."

Kitt raised a skeptical eyebrow again. "I don't think a good God would create a world with pain in it."

"Pain wasn't part of God's original plan. It *is* part of His plan for restoring His fallen world since Adam and Eve sinned. If we'll allow it, He'll use the sorrow and suffering in our lives to shape us into the image of Christ. Otherwise, we'll become brittle, hard and easily shattered by tragedies that come."

Kitt stilled as Polly talked. "I guess I have a choice to make, don't I?"

"It's not a one time choice, Kitt. It's a choice we have to make each time sorrow and pain come." Polly could hardly believe the words coming out of her mouth.

It's important to remember the power comes from the Holy Spirit, not from you. She smiled at the words Mother had spoken when they'd prayed together.

Thank you, Holy Spirit. I know the words aren't coming from me—I don't have that much wisdom. Thank you for helping me comfort Kitt with the same comfort you gave me.

♠

As Kitt headed for home, Polly's parents' voices mingled and wafted down from their bedroom window above Polly's head. She soaked up the joy of it from her seat on the porch steps. How wonderful to have two parents who loved her and loved each other.

When their voices quieted, Polly stood and stretched. She'd better—

"Florence, your mother isn't feeling well." Her father spoke through the screen door. "Would you go up and stay with her, please? I'm calling Dr. Cooley."

"Do you think she's in labor?"

"No, she's feeling sick to her stomach and has a bad headache. She's also spotting again."

Polly took the steps two at a time, then hurried to the back bedroom. She entered the room, thankful Father had darkened it so Mother could rest. She was lying on the bed, eyes closed, one hand pressed to her stomach. She clapped her other hand over her mouth. "I feel like I'm going to vomit. Get a bucket quick."

As Polly flew down the stairs, Father called to her. "Dr. Cooley is out on another home visit but his wife said he'll come as soon as he can. What are you doing?"

"Mother wanted a bucket. She thinks she's going to throw up." Polly grabbed a bucket in the kitchen, then raced up the stairs with Father close behind her.

"Bob! Bob! Florence!" Polly and her father dashed into the bedroom. "I can't see. I can't see."

Mother sat up, staring wildly around the room. The bucket had arrived too late, but they hardly noticed. She cried out again and her whole body stiffened, her back and neck arching. Her muscles jerked in a rhythmic pattern.

Polly tried to capture her mother's hands while her father gently pressed on her legs. "What's happening, Father?"

"I think she's having a seizure, but I don't know why. I don't know what to do."

Soon the jerking stopped and Mother collapsed on the bed.

"Margaret, Margaret." Father bent over his unresponsive wife and placed his ear on her chest.

"Is she breathing?" Polly tried to find a pulse on her mother's wrist as she'd seen Dr. Cooley do.

"I think so." Father's forehead puckered.

"She's alive. She has a pulse." Polly tried to count the beats.

Father stood up. "She's not conscious. I'm going to call Doc Cooley again. Maybe I can find out where he is."

As Father left the room, Polly trembled and her heart raced. Fear threatened to overtake her—fear of the unknown, fear of losing mother, fear of doing the wrong thing. Immediately, she began to pray. "Lord, you know what's wrong with Mother. Give Father and me wisdom and bring Dr. Cooley soon. Most of all give us peace and help us trust you even in this frightening time."

Be still and know that I am God. Polly sensed more than heard the words. Mother's prayer in this very room had been, "Fill it with your hope, your peace, and your joy, regardless of the circumstances."

"Yes, Lord." She cleaned Mother's dress as best she could.

Father came into the room and looked at Mother's still form on the bed. His shoulders slumped. "Lu Lu said Doc Cooley is in the country delivering a baby. She has no way to reach him because the family in the country has no phone. I'm going to go see if he can come."

Fear again tried to raise its ugly head. Father was going to leave her alone with Mother in this condition. What was the verse from Philippians Mother often quoted? "I can do all things through Christ who strengthens me." She could do this. She had to do this.

Mother stirred. She opened her eyes and looked around.

Polly held her breath. Could she see?

Wrinkling her nose, Mother looked at her soiled dress. "What happened?"

Polly exhaled as Father answered. "You weren't feeling well and when I went to call Dr. Cooley, you threw up and had a seizure." He tried to arrange Mother's pillows more comfortably.

"Oh, now I remember." Mother closed her eyes and settled deeper into her pillows. Then just as quickly, she opened her eyes wide, scanning the room. "I was blind. I couldn't see. Why was I blind?"

"We don't know." Polly stroked her mother's hands. "Dr. Cooley's out in the country delivering a baby. Father's going out to talk to him."

Mother barely nodded. Ordinarily, she would have said they shouldn't bother the doctor when he was delivering someone else's baby, but she said nothing.

Father kissed Mother's cheek, and then looked at Polly as he turned to leave the room. "Will you be all right, Shorty?"

He knew how hard this was for her. Willing her knees to stop shaking, she reached to squeeze his hand. "You go get Dr. Cooley. Don't worry about us."

CHAPTER 42

Bob rarely used the whip on his horses. Tonight he made an exception. His lovely wife's body jerking repeatedly during her seizure obsessed him as he pushed Jasper to speeds he had never attempted. At least not since he'd raced his father's horses when he was a boy.

Although he was a God-fearing man who attended church every Sunday, he mainly depended on his wife's prayers. He said grace at the table and he knew the Lord's Prayer. Faced with this kind of emergency, he didn't know how to approach the Sovereign of the universe.

Bob had been taught to believe in the absolute sovereignty of God, so did it even matter what he prayed? God was going to do what He wanted anyway, right? He'd always loved the simplicity of his wife's prayers. It seemed Margaret poured her heart out to God like a child, not worrying about whether her prayers fit in with some preconceived idea of what He was like.

Doesn't the Bible say unless we become like little children, we won't enter the kingdom of God? Maybe he needed to try Margaret's way of praying.

Still pushing his horse with unaccustomed fervor along the dark road, Bob began tentatively, "Father." Just saying the word made him feel better, his jaw muscles less tight, so he repeated it. "Father, I guess a grown man ought to know how to pray. I'm ashamed to say I've neglected that art. It's no excuse. It just hasn't seemed necessary because my wife is so skilled at praying."

His wife. She was so dear to him. Bob choked up and struggled to find words to express his deep emotion. "Father, you know how much I love Margaret. She's been an amazing wife and mother for more than 20 years. I don't know what I'd do without her."

Bob swallowed. "But I know enough from my Presbyterian catechism to know she doesn't belong to me. Job said you give and take away, and he knew it better than anyone. I know you're in control and you have a plan."

He peered at the lights ahead. Almost there. "I'm sorry I've neglected you for so long. Help me trust you no matter what happens."

Urging Jasper into one last burst of speed, Bob pulled up in front of the Smitley's rambling farmhouse behind Dr. Cooley's car. He yanked on the reins and leaped to the ground.. In a few quick strides, he reached the house and pounded on the door.

Mr. Smitley opened it, his brows drawing together when he saw Bob standing there. "What can I do for you, Bob? We're in the middle of a birthing here."

"I know, but my wife is in a bad way. I need to talk to Dr. Cooley."

"I'll see if he can come downstairs."

Bob shifted from one foot to the other and tried to smile at the brood of children huddled around the kitchen table. "Isn't it time for you all to be in bed?"

"Papa said we could stay up until the birthing's done if it doesn't take too long."

That must be Smitley's oldest boy.

Dr. Cooley rushed down the stairs, a scowl on his usually pleasant face. "What is it, Bob? Things aren't going well. I'm needed upstairs."

"It's Margaret, Doc. She... she went blind and then had a seizure or convulsion. Something is terribly wrong."

Dr Cooley's face lost color.

Bob grabbed his arm. "What is it?"

Sitting heavily on the bottom step, Dr. Cooley's eyes closed and wrinkles cut deep lines in his forehead. He looked very old. "I'm sorry, Bob. It sounds like eclampsia. I knew her blood pressure was too high off and on, but I thought we had it under control."

Mr. Smitley appeared at the top of the stairs, "Doc, we need you up here."

Dr. Cooley's shoulders sagged. "I'm working on a breech birth. I can't leave until Mabel delivers. I'll come as soon as I can."

Bob tried to swallow his panic. "What's eclampsia? What can we do?"

"I don't have time to explain. Keep her as comfortable as you can."

♠

Margaret took deep breaths. She needed to calm down instead of reliving the sheer terror of temporarily losing her sight and control of her body. *I'm not really in control anyway, Father. It's just an illusion. You're the One who's in control.* Margaret's pulse slowed. *Please help me not to give in to panic and fear. Fear was part of the unpleasant sensation Florence and I noticed in this room, and I don't want to open any doors we've closed through prayer.*

She glanced at her daughter. Florence's lips were moving, head bowed and eyes closed. Peace like a gentle breeze permeated the room. This was what she had prayed for, that Florence would have a relationship with God that was truly her own, that her faith would be strong enough to uphold her when Margaret's life was over. Her prayer was being answered. There was just one thing she needed to ask her daughter.

♠

Polly looked up to find her mother watching her with love-filled eyes, and something else Polly couldn't fathom. Sadness? "What is it, Mother?"

Mother reached out to take Polly's hand in her own. "Florence, there's something I need to ask you."

Polly waited, her muscles tightening.

"If anything should happen to me... if I don't come through this delivery..."

"No, Mother. Don't say that." Polly pulled away and covered her face with her hands.

"Only God knows the future. We're not in control."

Tears dripped down Polly's wrists as her mother reached again to take her hand.

"If anything should happen to me, will you help your father raise the children? I know I'm asking a lot."

Polly shook with repressed sobs as she nodded. "You know you needn't ask, Mama. I've always been committed to my family. That's partly why Garrett and I argued so much. He knew my family came first—perhaps he knew it always would."

Mother leaned over to kiss Polly's cheek.

"Mama, please don't give up. We don't even know what's wrong with you. Maybe it's nothing serious."

Smiling and patting Polly's hand before withdrawing her own, Mother shook her head. "I haven't given up, but I think we both know this is serious. Whatever it is."

Horses' hooves clattered on the road outside the window, then the door opened and closed downstairs. "Don't say anything to your father, Florence. He'll just worry and fret even more."

Polly nodded as her father's footsteps thudded on the stairs. In the hall, he talked to someone in low tones before he came into the room.

"How are you, Margaret?" He took Mother's hands in his.

"I haven't had any more seizures or episodes of blindness, so I guess—"

"Where is Dr. Cooley?" Polly peered into the nursery.

Father bit his lip and shook his head. "He's in the middle of a breech birth and can't come until the baby is delivered."

"Did you talk to him? Did you tell him what happened?" Polly's voice rasped with frustration.

Father's shoulders drooped. "I did, but he can't leave in the middle of a breech birth. He said we just need to keep her as comfortable as possible until he gets here."

"I understand." Mother's tone was so gentle compared to hers. "Did Dr. Cooley attempt any sort of diagnosis?"

"It was a word I'd never heard before." Father hesitated. "Something like *clampsa*."

"Eclampsia," Margaret whispered. "I should have known. Mrs. Morgan had that."

Father's eyes bulged. "Mrs. Morgan *died*."

CHAPTER 43

Polly cringed at her father's outburst, but Mother nodded. "Dr. Cooley did all he could but it's a very serious condition."

A shudder passed through Mother's body as she finished speaking. Polly stood up, fearing another seizure. Mother shook her head. "I think my labor has begun, and that's a good thing. With eclampsia, the more quickly the baby is delivered, the better."

Father had sunk into a chair with his head in his hands. At Mother's words, he sprang to his feet. "I'm going to call Dr. Wilson in Franklin. He did good work the short time he took over Dr. Cooley's practice."

Following him out of the room, Polly went to get a basin of cool water and a washcloth. Anything was better than sitting here feeling helpless. She stopped and listened at the bedroom doors. Not a sound. The little ones must be settled for the night.

On her way back to Mother's room, basin and washcloth in hand, Polly reached the top of the stairs just as Ben and Maggie opened their doors. Ben frowned at her. "What's going on with Mother?"

Polly sighed and shook her head. Praying for wisdom, she gave Maggie and Ben a toned-down version of what was happening.

Maggie stared at Polly. "Is Mother going to be all right?"

Polly dropped her gaze, looking at the basin and washcloth in her hands. "Only God knows for sure."

Ben squared his shoulders. His lips trembled. "Is there anything we can do?"

"Just pray and keep the children out of Mother's room. I don't want them to be frightened."

Hurrying to the back bedroom, she heard muffled groans. Mother had one arm flung across her eyes and her other hand pressing on her abdomen. She sat up, gagging, then pressed her lips together. Polly grabbed the bucket and held it under Mother's chin. "It's okay if you need to throw up."

Her own stomach churned, and Polly prayed she wouldn't lose her dinner as Mother vomited again. *Please, Father, don't let me fail Mother now.*

Rushing into the room, her father gulped. Mother had always cleaned up when one of the children was sick because he had a weak stomach.

When Mother's nausea passed, Polly rearranged her pillows to make her comfortable. She looked at Father. "What did you find out?"

"Dr. Wilson is on his way. He has a car and will be here as soon as he can."

Polly breathed a sigh of relief. Help was on its—

Mother's back arched and her body began the rhythmic jerks just as it had before. Father knelt beside her and tried to support her while Polly ran to the other side of the bed. Her father looked like Polly felt—helpless.

♠

As he paced in front of the bedroom window, Bob paused before each turn and stared into the darkness. After what seemed like an eternity, the wheels of Dr. Wilson's car crunched and a car door slammed. Much as Bob disliked the noisy backfires that always accompanied motor vehicles, Dr. Wilson had arrived much quicker than if he'd been depending on horses.

Bob ran down the stairs, across the living room and threw open the door just as Dr. Wilson started to knock. "Come in and do hurry. Margaret isn't doing well and Dr. Cooley hasn't arrived."

"Tell me exactly what symptoms she's having." Dr. Wilson headed for the steps.

Bob described Margaret's condition as they climbed.

"Has Margaret's labor begun?"

"Yes, her contractions started a few hours ago. What can you do?"

"Various things, but to be honest, none of them work very well. The medical profession is divided on it. Since seizures cut off oxygen to the baby's brain, I'll try to stop them with morphine while I also give her nitroglycerine to bring down her blood pressure."

Dr. Wilson used a handkerchief to wipe sweat from his brow as they dashed down the hall. "A Cesarean section is also often recommended, but very difficult in a home setting." He entered the back bedroom, Bob following.

Both men stopped just inside the doorway. Margaret was having another seizure.

♠

Surely hours had passed as Polly tried to assist Dr. Wilson. Nothing he'd done brought much change in Mother's condition. So many seizures. How could the baby survive?

Dr. Wilson had sent Father downstairs after he'd thrown up in Mother's bucket. Polly wasn't doing well either. She clenched her teeth and swallowed down the waves of nausea. *There was a reason I wasn't a nurse.*

"I didn't want to do a Cesarean section—it's so risky outside an operating room." Dr. Wilson kept his voice low as he wiped his forehead with the small white towel Polly had given him. "Let's take another look." He passed Polly a flashlight to shine as he examined Mother.

He raised his voice. "Hang on, Margaret, we're almost there. The baby's head is crowning. Try to push now. " Dr. Wilson gripped Mother's hand.

Polly loved him for his gentleness with her mother who was barely conscious. One more weak push, and Dr. Wilson held a perfectly formed but very silent baby boy. She watched as he tied off the umbilical cord.

Babies were supposed to cry, weren't they? He didn't even make a sound when Dr. Wilson gave him a spank on his bottom. *Come on, breathe, breathe.*

After a few more minutes of unfruitful labor, Dr. Wilson handed the infant to Polly, his eyes red rimmed. "I'm so sorry. He must have been deprived of oxygen for too long. Wrap the little one in a blanket."

Polly reached for the baby as Dr. Wilson finished the afterbirth process with her mother. A tear trickled down her nose as she wrapped his still form in one of the blankets Mother had prepared.

At last the doctor turned toward the door. "I'll go tell your father."

"What about Mother?"

Dr. Wilson studied Mother whose eyes were still closed, her chest rising and falling. "She's so sound asleep from the morphine. Let's wait until she wakes up to tell her about the baby. She's had a rough night."

CHAPTER 44

For the first time in a very long while, Savannah woke with a song in her heart. The dark cloud was gone and the sun streamed through her window. She stretched and sat up in bed. Why was she so happy?

Ah, yes. Last night Garrett's mother had treated her like a real person. Savannah sprang out of bed and dressed in her most modest, lime green dress. When Mrs. Young had prayed God would heal Savannah's wounded heart and give her a new beginning, she had allowed herself to cry for the first time in years. With every tear that fell, the hardness of her heart softened, opening the door of her inner being to His love.

In addition to helping Savannah find work, Mrs. Young had said she'd help her find a room. Savannah shook her head. Why would anyone do this for her? Her mother had always assured her that people would be able to tell immediately that Savannah was no good, but Mrs. Young didn't seem to see her that way.

Savannah went to her vanity, picked up her hairbrush, and gazed deep into her eyes. "I am a new creature in Christ. Old things have passed away—all things have become new." That's what Mrs. Young had told her. Savannah intended to keep saying it until she believed it to the depths of her soul.

She took a deep breath. "Today is the first day of my new life."

♠

Garrett wasn't sure how his mother had managed it. She had persuaded his father to give Savannah a job working in his office, even though she had no experience doing office work. Pa said sometimes that was best because then he didn't have to "untrain" people before he trained them.

Whistling as he ran down the steps, he saluted his mother standing in the hall talking on the telephone. He poured himself a glass of orange juice from the icebox and sipped it slowly.

"Savannah's been through a lot, but she's a new creature in Christ now."

Ma must be talking to Mrs. Patton. Garrett smiled. The Lord could change anyone, even him.

"I heard you were looking for someone to help with light housekeeping at your boarding house. Could Savannah do that in exchange for room and board? Do you think that would be fair, Innis?"

Garrett took another sip of orange juice. Maybe Mrs. Patton would be more apt to help someone who'd gone through hard times since she'd gone through rough times herself when she'd divorced her husband. Now that she ran the Sandy Lake boarding house, she'd be in a position to help Savannah.

He tried to read his mother's expression when she came into the kitchen. "Good morning, Ma." Garrett kissed his mother's cheek and smiled into her eyes.

"I wanted to tell you how much I appreciate what you're doing for Savannah. I can't think of anyone else's mother who'd be willing to risk her own reputation to help someone like her. You're the best."

Ma patted his cheek. "It's the right thing to do. Jesus said, *Inasmuch as you did it to one of the least of these..., you did it to Me.*"

"Is Mrs. Patton going to rent a room to Savannah?"

Ma's brows drew together. "She will, but under very strict conditions."

"What conditions?"

"There will be a trial period of six months. If Savannah keeps her part of the bargain and helps with light housekeeping chores, Mrs. Patton will charge her just half the normal daily rate." Ma went to the cupboard to get some plates. "*But,* if Savannah entertains a gentleman caller in her room even *once,* she will have to leave immediately. Mrs. Patton runs a respectable establishment. She can't afford to have her reputation ruined."

The tension released from Garrett's shoulders and he took a swallow of juice. "That's more than fair. I'm sure Savannah will understand the need for a trial period. Most people wouldn't be willing to take the risk in the first place."

"Mrs. Patton knows what it's like to be looked down on." His mother got some silverware from a drawer.

Garrett nodded. "I'm sure she does."

"Your father said this morning that Savannah can start work as soon as she moves to Sandy Lake." Ma started setting the table. "Mrs. Patton's rooms are furnished, so she won't need anything aside from clothing and the like."

"That's great. I think I'll skip breakfast this morning so I can tell Savannah the good news on my way to work."

"At least take a cinnamon roll to eat on the way—take one for Savannah, too."

♠

A shuddering sigh escaped Polly's lips as Father and Dr. Wilson came into the back bedroom. She laid the tiny, blanket-wrapped form in her father's arms, biting her lips to hold back her sobs. Tears slid down his cheeks as he gazed at his son.

Polly looked at the clock. The darkened windows in her parents' bedroom hid the fact that it was already morning, but the clock told her soon they would have to tell Mother her precious baby had died.

Father and Dr. Wilson were talking in quiet tones when a car backfired as it stopped in front of their house. Polly walked to the window and lifted the shade. "Dr. Cooley is here."

Dr Wilson nodded. "I'll go talk to him."

Still holding the tiny bundle, her father looked as though he didn't know what to do with it.

"I'm sorry, Father. We tried so hard to save the baby. I know how much you wanted another boy."

Father didn't respond or resist when Polly gently took the baby and put him in the crib in the adjoining room. As she returned to the back bedroom, a single tear rolled down his cheek. If only Mother were awake, she would know how to comfort him. No, Mother would need comforting too when she woke up.

Good manners took her downstairs to thank the doctors, even as she sent up a silent prayer. *Holy Spirit, Mother says you're the Comforter. Please comfort my parents in this loss, console all of us. I don't know what to do.*

As Polly approached the bottom of the stairs, the two doctors were arguing but keeping their voices low.

"Chloroform would have been a better choice than morphine. Maybe the morphine caused the baby's death." Dr. Cooley's face was red.

"Let me remind you seizures deprive the baby of oxygen, so it's in the best interest of the child to use morphine to stop the seizures."

"But—"

They stopped talking as Polly entered the room. She turned to Dr. Cooley. "Thank you for coming. We called Dr. Wilson because Mother's condition was so serious, and we didn't know when you'd be able to come."

"I'm sorry I couldn't be here, Polly. I couldn't leave Mrs. Smitley in her condition."

"We understand. Dr. Wilson did everything possible. There were so many seizures we feared for the lives of Mother and the baby."

"How is Margaret?" Dr. Cooley turned toward the stairs.

"She was exhausted from labor and the repeated seizures, so I thought it best not to tell her of the baby's death until she'd slept awhile." Dr. Wilson took out a clean, white handkerchief and mopped his forehead. "Polly, why don't you and your father try to get some sleep, and I'll sit with your mother awhile to make sure she's okay."

"That won't be necessary." Dr. Cooley's tone was brusque. "I'll have my nurse come over and stay."

Polly wavered, torn between wanting to stay with her mother and wanting to sleep. She sagged against the wall. "I guess that would be best. I don't know if I can get through this day without any sleep." She stifled a yawn. "But the children will be up soon—"

"Maggie and Ben can look after the children." Dr. Cooley patted her arm. "May I use your telephone, Polly?"

"Of course." Polly pointed the way and then with a final thank you to Dr. Wilson, she went into the sitting room. Tears poured down her cheeks as soon as the door closed behind her.

CHAPTER 45

Margaret opened her eyes and looked around the darkened room. Someone had drawn the shades against the sun but it still filtered in here and there. What time was it? What day was it? She touched her stomach, still swollen but flatter than before. The baby. The baby had been born at last. So many seizures she'd had. No wonder she was exhausted.

Where was the baby? She didn't even know if she'd had a boy or a girl. Wouldn't the little one be hungry by now? Had the morphine made her sleep so soundly she'd slept right through the baby's cries?

"Can I get you anything, Mrs. Dye?"

Margaret was amazed at how quietly Nurse Dayton had come to the side of her bed for all her considerable size. "I didn't know you were here."

"Dr. Cooley asked me to stay for a couple hours to make sure you're all right. He tells me you had a difficult time. Eclampsia is a formidable foe."

"It was a long, black night and I didn't know if I'd see the dawn. Can you bring me my baby? Did I have a boy or a girl?"

Nurse Dayton lowered herself into the chair she'd pulled next to the bed. "Margaret." She took Margaret's hands, her voice gentle. "Your baby boy didn't live. The seizures must have kept him from getting oxygen. He never drew his first birth. I'm so sorry, dearie."

Margaret squeezed her eyes shut, tears rolling down her cheeks, shoulders shaking. No, not her sweet baby. How would she fill the emptiness that Nurse Dayton's words had created in her heart? If only she could go back to sleep and awaken to find it had been a bad dream. But she wasn't dreaming. She opened her eyes. "Where is he? Can I see him?"

"Do you think it's a good idea, dearie?"

Taking a deep breath, Margaret nodded. "I need to see him."

"I'll try to get him without waking Mr. Dye. He needs his rest."

Miss Dayton re-entered the room before Margaret could prepare her heart. She reached to take the small-blanketed form nonetheless. Folding the blanket back, she looked at the perfect features of her ninth child. He was smaller than her other babies, with long eyelashes brushing his cold cheeks, tiny hands balled into fists.

"Oh Father," she sobbed as she clutched the baby to her breast, her whole body shaking. "You promised..." Her tears washed down over the delicate features of her son. "You promised your grace *is* sufficient for me. I'm taking you at your Word." She gazed again at the tiny features. "The spirit of this little one is already in heaven with you, and he will never experience the joys or the sorrows that would have been his if he'd lived. Help me and the rest of the family not to grieve as those who have no hope."

Margaret bowed her head. Job had lost *all* his children in one day and yet had not sinned by charging God with any wrongdoing. Softly she whispered, "The Lord gave and the Lord has taken away; blessed be the name of the Lord."

More tears spilled down her cheeks. At last she handed the wee one back to the nurse. "Could you put him in the cradle over there in the corner? I don't want the children to find him in the nursery."

As the nurse took the baby, Margaret added, "You don't need to stay. I'd like to be alone for awhile. Bob will be awake soon."

"If you're sure then, Margaret."

As the door closed behind the nurse, Margaret crumpled onto her pillows, her sobs shaking the entire bed.

♠

With a muffled groan, Polly raised one eyelid. Twila's bright eyes peered at her while she patted Polly's cheek. In spite of her weariness, Polly couldn't scold her. She tried to stifle a yawn as she kissed Twila. "Good morning, Little One."

Twila put her head affectionately on Polly's chest and stuck her thumb in her mouth—a habit she had regained recently.

"Where's Maggie?"

Twila pulled out her thumb and pointed toward the door. "Kitchen. Make lunch."

"Lunch? I must have slept longer than I thought. I'd better go change my clothes."

"Me come?"

"All right. You can come." Polly swooped Twila up. She had never been able to deny her baby sister when Twila looked at her with those sparkling blue eyes.

As they walked up the stairs, Mother shouted. "Bob... Florence..." Polly's heart sped up. What now?

"Mama?" Twila's eyes grew wide.

Polly deposited her on the steps. "Go find Maggie. Mama's calling and I need to know you're safe. Okay?"

With trembling lips and tearful eyes, Twila nodded and started down the stairs, step by step.

Waiting long enough to be sure Twila obeyed, Polly took the stairs two at a time, arriving in her parents' room just seconds behind her father.

He scanned the room "What's wrong? Where's Nurse Dayton?"

"I thought I was okay, so I told her to go home. I don't know what's wrong." Mother shook her head and then gripped it between her hands. "I don't feel good. I'm cold and dizzy—sick to my stomach."

Father rushed to kneel beside the bed. "Polly, call Dr. Cooley and tell him to come right away. Hurry."

Polly dashed down the stairs and dialed the number as quickly as her shaking hands would allow, willing Dr. Cooley to answer. Instead his wife's voice said, "Cooley residence." "Hello, Mrs. Cooley. It's Polly Dye. Mama isn't feeling well. She sent Nurse Dayton home. Can the doctor come right away? I know he's had a long night."

After hearing Mrs. Cooley's affirmative answer, Polly hung up and turned to see Maggie and Ben staring at her with wide eyes. "I can't talk now..."

Ben grabbed her hand. "Why haven't we heard a baby crying and what's wrong with Mama?"

Hanging her head, Polly guided her siblings into Mama's sitting room to tell them the sad news.

♠

Polly had never seen Dr. Cooley move so quickly as he rushed to Mother's side. He looked at her still, white face. "How long has she been like this?"

"She lost consciousness soon after we called you." Father's eyes never left Dr. Cooley's face. "What is it? Eclampsia again?"

Dr. Cooley grabbed his black bag and rifled through it for his stethoscope and blood pressure cuff. Taking Mother's limp arm in his hand, he quickly attached the cuff. Almost immediately, he dropped it and pulled back the covers. "Oh no. Please, not this."

Dr. Cooley's body had blocked Polly's view, but as he moved to pick up his black bag again, she saw the pools of blood and gasped. Mother was bleeding, perhaps had been bleeding for some time.

Polly couldn't breathe. The room grew dim and whirled, then righted itself as sobs shook her whole body. "Why—Why didn't—Why didn't she tell us she was bleeding?"

"I'm sure she didn't know." Dr. Cooley worked feverishly doing an internal exam behind the sheets. "The trauma her body has been through must have kept her from sensing what was happening."

"Why is she bleeding? This never happened before." Father clenched and unclenched his fists, averting his white face.

"Sometimes it's caused by fragments of the placenta or amniotic sac that weren't expelled during childbirth. I'm checking now, but I'm not finding anything."

Polly squeezed her eyes shut and swallowed hard. Beside her Father swallowed repeatedly and took in loud gulps of air. Why couldn't they put aside their weak stomachs and focus on the seriousness of Mother's condition? If only Nurse Dayton had stayed, maybe she'd have checked Mother for bleeding.

"Margaret's labor went on so long because of all the complications. I suspect the uterus is no longer contracting. That's another cause of post partum hemorrhaging."

Usually, Dr. Cooley spoke in terms normal people could understand. Polly had never heard some of these words. She opened her eyes and moved around Dr. Cooley to take Mother's hand.

His forehead wrinkled, the doctor muttered to himself. "I'll try putting direct pressure on the aorta first..." He looked up at Polly. "Go call Nurse Dayton. Tell her I need her immediately." Then he noticed his friend's white face for the first time. "Bob, you'd better hustle out of here before I have two unconscious people."

CHAPTER 46

Maggie had never seen the children so subdued. No one wanted to eat after Dr. Cooley arrived, but at her insistence, they nibbled at the peanut butter and King syrup sandwiches she prepared. Afterward, she suggested a nap for the younger girls but Twila and Elsie set up such a howl that she allowed them to stay up as long as they behaved. She herself wouldn't have wanted to be banished at a time like this.

Now they all sat together in the living room. Even Father and Polly had joined them when Dr. Cooley chased them out of Mother's room. Was this what the valley of the shadow of death looked like?

Father took a deep breath and motioned the younger children to come closer. "I have..." He gulped. "I have... some very sad news." His voice cracked on the last words. He closed his eyes, then opened them again. "Your little brother... Your little brother...died."

The children's faces showed their degree of understanding as Father explained their brother's death, having to stop often to clear his throat and wipe his eyes. Twila and Elsie had wide eyes and wrinkled foreheads, while the other children blinked hard or wiped their own eyes.

Polly buried her face in her hands as he spoke. Elsie patted her hands and Twila wiped her tears and murmuring, "Polly cwy. Polly cwy." Maggie put her arm around Polly.

Raising her head, Polly gazed at Maggie. "If only I could have saved him. If only there had been *something* I could do."

"Would the baby have lived if Dr. Cooley had been here?" George's voice cracked.

"I don't think so. Dr. Wilson is a very good doctor, but sometimes even the best doctors can't save a life." Father swallowed and drew a deep breath. "Dr. Cooley is working with Mother upstairs. She isn't doing well. She's been unconscious for some time."

"What's 'unconscious,' Papa?" Beth gazed at her father.

"It's like being asleep but no one can wake you." Polly buried her face in her hands again.

Maggie peered at the clock. One-thirty—an hour since Nurse Dayton had arrived. "Father, may I ask Dr. Cooley how Mother is doing?"

Father agreed. He looked at Robert and Ben who had been sitting like stumps on the floor. "Are you boys okay?"

They nodded but didn't meet Father's eyes.

Maggie tiptoed up the stairs even though the noise of her footsteps couldn't bother Mother if she was still unconscious. Maybe she had rallied and Maggie would have good news for the family.

She tapped lightly on her parents' door, and after a minute or two, Nurse Dayton opened it. "What is it, Maggie?"

"We were wondering if there's any change in Mother's condition?"

"I'm afraid she's still unconscious and still hemorrhaging. Dr. Cooley is doing all he can. We'll let you know if there's any change."

As Maggie trudged down the stairs, she brushed a tear from her cheek.

♠

Footsteps tripped up the cement stairs in the front yard. Polly glanced out the window as Blanche Davis walked across the porch. She sprang to her feet and met her at the door. Blanche held a fragrant earthenware casserole which she handed to Polly. "I saw cars at your house yesterday and today. Is everything okay? How's your mother doing?"

Glancing at her family, Polly handed the casserole to Maggie, who had followed her, and stepped out on the porch, closing the door. She wasn't sure the family could handle another rendition of the baby's death and their mother's unstable condition. She wasn't sure she could.

Polly swallowed hard. "I'm sorry not to invite you in, Blanche." Her voice trembled. "Things are bad." She bit her lip and pressed her hand to her mouth.

"Oh, Polly, what happened?"

"Mother developed eclampsia last night—"

"What's eclampsia?"

Between shuddering breaths, Polly tried to explain the condition she'd never heard of until yesterday. "That's probably what caused my baby brother's death."

Blanche's lips trembled. Was she remembering the death of her own babies?

"Then today, after we thought Mother was okay, she started bleeding. She's been unconscious for a couple of hours. Dr. Cooley thinks..." Polly hesitated. "He thinks her uterus isn't retracting."

"Contracting? I'm so sorry."

Tears streamed down Polly's face, and Blanche reached out to touch her cheek. "I know what it's like to lose people you love. I'll be praying for you and your family. Let me know if there's anything else I can do."

Polly took deep breaths as Blanche headed down the front walkway. This was a normal Saturday for everyone around them but for her and her family, time seemed to have stopped. She wiped tears and some sweat from her forehead. It was going to be hot again today, but no amount of heat could penetrate the chill working its way into her heart.

Was it just last night her mother asked her to take care of the children if she didn't come through the delivery?

"No, Heavenly Father," she whispered. "Please no. I don't feel nearly wise enough to take on that job. Please don't take her from us. We need her so much."

In the silence, a light breeze ruffled Polly's unruly hair, tumbled and uncombed since the day before. Then she sensed more than heard, "Be still and know that I am God. I will never leave you nor forsake you."

Polly closed her eyes, wanting to hold on to the comfort in those words. But God had made no promises about her mother.

Part of her wanted to beg Him to tell her what was going to happen, even as part of her shrank from knowing.

A small voice spoke behind her. "Polly awight?"

Her youngest sister peered through the screen, blue eyes squinting and a frown on her forehead. Polly opened the door and pulled Twila into her arms. "I'm not sure who is taking care of whom here, Little One. Perhaps right now I need you more than you need me."

Twila put her chubby arms around her sister's neck and squeezed with all her might. "Love Polly."

"I love you, too."

If something happened to their precious mother, they were all going to need each other more than ever. Mother had been the glue that held their family together. What would become of them if she died? *Oh God, please don't let our family fall apart the way the Davis family did when Sarah died.*

She and Twila went back indoors. Polly noticed the clock. Only two-thirty. The hours dragged.

"Papa, may I go up and check on Mama?" Beth's big blue eyes were wide and appealing. "I want to be a nurse when I grow up. I don't think I'd get sick to my stomach."

Father shook his head. "No, I'm sorry. Dr. Cooley said he'd come tell us if there's any change."

Heavy footsteps started down the stairs. Slow, plodding footsteps. Every head turned toward the doorway at the bottom of the stairs, waiting.

Dr. Cooley entered the room, his brow wrinkled and face unsmiling. He shook his head and spoke in a low voice. "I'm sorry, Bob. I'm so sorry. We did everything we could but she'd lost—" He looked at the children and pressed his lips together. "Nurse Dayton is.... She will..."

No, No, No! Oh, God, no. Please, God, no. Polly gripped Twila even more fiercely. She couldn't allow herself to lose control. Tears poured down her cheeks.

"Father." She choked and coughed, and then tried again. "Why don't you and Dr. Cooley go into the sitting room to talk?"

When the men left the room, Beth and Maggie began to sob, and tears ran down the boys' faces—even Ben's. Only Twila and

Elsie were dry-eyed. Polly struggled for composure as she sat down and pulled Elsie up on her lap too.

She gazed deep into Twila's eyes and then Elsie's. "Mama was very, very sick. She was so sick Dr. Cooley couldn't make her better, so she went to be with Jesus and our little brother."

"When Mama come back?" Elsie squinted at Polly.

"Mama can't come back, Sweetie. But I promised her I'd help Papa take care of you if she couldn't. She loved you all so much."

Polly leaned back, fished a handkerchief out of her pocket, wiped her eyes and blew her nose a few times. She tried to smile at her brothers and sisters.

"We have each other. That's what's important, and Mama would want us to stick together."

But how could a family *stick together* when the glue that had held it was gone?

CHAPTER 47

As Polly came downstairs from settling Twila and Elsie for their naps, she found Father and Dr. Cooley leaving the front room. They shook hands wordlessly and Dr. Cooley walked to his car, shoulders slumped, head bowed.

"Nurse Dayton is preparing Mother's body..." Father's voice broke. He scrubbed his hand over his eyes. "She's preparing Mother's body for burial, Florence. Maybe you could pick out a dress?"

When Polly nodded, he added, "Dr. Cooley will ask Reverend Lawrence if he can help us plan the service. It will have to be soon. We'll just have it at the house. I think that's what your mother would have wanted."

Getting out his handkerchief, Father sighed and blew his nose. "We thought we'd have many years to plan our funeral services. I can't believe she's gone. Only last night we walked down Broad Street together."

Polly could find no words of comfort for her father. Her own pain was too great. She nodded as inwardly she cried out to the Holy Spirit. *Holy Spirit, please, please comfort my Papa.*

Glancing around the empty room, Father slumped into Mother's favorite chair. "Where is everyone?"

"I put Twila and Elsie to bed, Ben is outside with Robert and George, and Maggie went for a walk with Beth." Polly hugged her father as she used to as a child. "I'll find a dress for Mother."

Feet dragging, Polly mounted the stairs. No reason for speed now as there had been the other times she'd flown up and down these steps in the past weeks.

Rubbing her throbbing head, she hesitated, then pushed open the door to her parents' bedroom. Would Mother look different now that her spirit had gone to be with Jesus?

Nurse Dayton, brisk and efficient, was bent over washing Mother's arms and hands in her usual no-nonsense way. *Thank God.* If Nurse Dayton had been squeamish about her task, Polly didn't know what she would have done.

Polly stood, feet glued to the floor, eyes fixed on Mother's pale, drawn face. *Our bodies are just the houses we live in until our Father calls us home.* Mother had told her that when her beloved Aunt Mary died when Polly was small.

"Polly." The nurse's voice was gentle. "Did you come to say good bye to your mother?"

Good bye? *No.* She wasn't ready to say good bye. Would she ever be ready? "No." Polly's voice wavered. She cleared her throat. "Father asked me to pick a dress for Mother. Is there anything I can do to help you?"

"No, dearie, you've gone through quite enough."

Polly blew out a relieved breath and stood in front of the hooks by the door which held Mother's dresses. There weren't many choices. Her old brown work dress and two less shabby green ones. One dark blue Sunday dress. Polly pulled out the dress she'd heard her mother describe as "dove gray" that she wore for special occasions. As she held it, the faint hint of lavender her mother used when dressing up almost undid her. Tears rolled down Polly's cheeks. This was the last special occasion for which her mother would ever dress up.

Sniffing hard, Polly carried the dress to Nurse Dayton who was pulling a clean sheet over Mother's body. "Is this all right?"

"That will be perfect. Your mother wore this dress for church once or twice and at your Uncle Joe's wedding. I'm sure she would have picked it if she'd had the opportunity."

Pressing her cheek against the silky fabric, Polly closed her eyes and then handed the dress to Nurse Dayton. "I'd better see if Father needs me."

"You run along."

Stopping outside her bedroom where Twila and Elsie were sleeping, Polly put her ear to the door. All was quiet. She almost envied the girls being too little to understand their family's loss. On the other hand, when they grew up, they might not have any memories of their mother. *I can't let that happen. I have to make sure we keep the girls' memories of Mother alive.*

When she stepped into the living room, her father sat alone on the couch, staring bleakly into space, barely acknowledging Polly's presence. He so seldom did nothing.

"Father." Polly sat down beside him. "Is Pastor Lawrence coming?"

"He'll be here as soon as he can."

When her father continued to stare into space, Polly touched his arm. "We're going to get through this, Papa. We will. I promised Mama I'd help you raise the children if anything should happen to her."

Her father looked up. "When was that?"

"When you went to get Dr. Cooley."

"That's a big responsibility." Father studied Polly's face. "What about Garrett?"

"You know Garrett's not interested in me."

"Are you sure about that? People can change their minds."

"I was sad when we broke up, but I knew he wasn't the one. He's in love with someone else anyway."

A knock on the front door brought Father to his feet. "That must be the pastor. Would you stay and help us plan the service?"

"Of course. We could sit at the dining room table."

As her father greeted their pastor, he expressed his sympathy, his eyes kind and his voice gentle. She'd always thought he was at his best when someone had suffered a loss.

In spite of Polly's efforts to be strong for her father, Reverend Lawrence's kindness got past her defenses. She had to tell him her secret fears. "Pastor, I have to admit I'm worried about our family. I've always thought Mother was the glue that held us together. Now that she's gone, I'm afraid we'll fall apart."

Pastor Lawrence smiled at Polly. "Your mother was a wonderful person but God's Word says it's the power of God that holds everything together."

Polly's eyes widened. "Does it really say that?"

"It does. Maybe in the past, the power of God worked through your mother to hold this family together, but it was still

His power. Continue to put your trust in Him, and He will continue to be the glue."

"Thank you, Pastor. God has been teaching me to trust Him. Still I didn't expect to be tested so soon."

"It is a huge test, Polly. But it's wonderful God has been preparing you."

Polly nodded. God had taught her so much from the pages of Sarah's diary and from Blanche who had told her the rest of the story. "I'd have to say it was Sarah's legacy to me."

Reverend Lawrence raised his eyebrows. "Sarah's legacy?"

Polly shook her head. "Some day I'll tell you the story."

CHAPTER 48

When Polly heard the birds chirping on Sunday morning, she could barely open her eyes. A huge lump in her chest made breathing hard and a cry pushed against her lips. *Oh God...* Would waking up be like this for the rest of her life?

Oh God... How could you take my mother? How could you do that to us? Maybe it is your power that holds all things together and maybe this is a test for me, but I don't care. I just want my mother.

Polly ached all over but the ache in her heart engulfed her. How in the world would she get through this day, let alone the rest of her life? How could she help Father raise this family with her own emotions raw and raging?

Rustling sounds and whimpers came from the room Twila and Elsie had been sharing with Maggie and Beth. The little ones would soon be calling her name. If she waited for Maggie to respond to them, it was likely Beth's sleep would be disturbed. Stifling a groan, Polly rolled over, sat up, and faced the first of what would surely be many bleak days.

♠

Holding Twila in her right arm while keeping the fingers of her left hand lightly on Elsie's shoulder, Polly went to the door. She'd heard only a knock, no sound of an automobile or horses' hooves, so she wasn't surprised to see Kitt through the screen. She stood on the porch with a covered dish in her hands.

"Thank you for coming, Kitt."

"It looks like you have your hands full with the girls, so just tell me where to put this salad." Kitt opened the screen door.

"Probably in the ice box if it needs to be kept cool. Let's see if there's room. Reverend Lawrence's wife made phone calls asking people to bring meals. Mother had so many friends, and they're all bringing food."

"I'm so sorry about your mother." Kitt swiped at her eyes. "I can't believe she's gone."

Polly nodded. "It's like a nightmare except I can't wake up."

Kitt looked deep into Polly's eyes. "Do you remember the conversation you and I had a few days ago about suffering? Now it's my turn to comfort you."

"Thank you, Kitt." Polly tried to smile but her facial muscles wouldn't respond.

Kitt made a place in the icebox for the salad, and then followed Polly into the sitting room. She held out her arms to Elsie who went to her willingly. Polly settled herself and Twila on the sofa and motioned for Kitt and Elsie to join them.

"How are you doing?" Kitt eased herself and Elsie onto the davenport and reached for Polly's hand.

"I woke up so angry at God." Polly pulled her hand away and pounded the sofa. "How could He take my mother when we need her so much? Eight of us now without a mother."

"That's how I felt for a long time after my father died, until you helped me."

Polly frowned. "*I* helped you?

"Yes. Remember when you said we all have a choice to make every time we experience sorrow and pain?"

Polly closed her eyes, trying to shut out Kitt's words.

"You said we have to choose whether we'll allow God to use our sorrow and pain to shape us into the image of Christ, or whether we'll become brittle and easily shattered by the tragedies we experience."

Kitt touched Polly's arm. "You helped me so much, Polly. I went home and thought a lot about what you said. I decided I didn't want to become brittle and hard—I could already feel it happening. So I asked God to take away my bitterness and anger and give me the comfort and strength I needed."

Polly looked out the window at the sunshine that mocked her grief. "It was easier saying that to you when I wasn't the one suffering. I miss my mother." She glared at Kitt. "How will I survive without her?"

"I'm praying the Holy Spirit will comfort you and your family, Polly. I know He comforted me when you prayed for me, and I believe He'll do the same for you." Kitt hugged Elsie close. "You said Sarah Davis never turned against God even though she'd lost five children, and I'm praying God will strengthen you just as He strengthened her."

Polly's eyes widened. She could hardly believe the words coming from her friend's lips. Almost overnight, the student had become the teacher.

Kitt got to her feet, still holding Elsie. "Mother offered to watch Twila and Elsie for awhile so you can have a break. Why don't you let me take them now?"

Let the little ones out of her sight? She fought the panic that quickened her pulse. "That's so good of your mother." She hugged Twila tight. What about her promise to Mother? But Sarah's clinging rather than trusting had not produced good results in her children. Polly loosened her grip. "Maybe I'll take her up on her offer if you're sure it isn't too much trouble."

"Not at all. It will be nice to have some children in our house again."

As soon as Kitt and the girls left, Polly surveyed the quiet house and headed for the stairs. Maggie and Beth were curled up on their bed reading and barely looked up as Polly picked up her Bible and Sarah's diary. "Kitt came to take Elsie and Twila to their house for awhile. I'm taking a walk."

♠

Peace replaced Polly's panic as she walked and took deep breaths. She had needed to get away from the house—to be alone. She followed the well-worn path to the creek and settled herself beside it. The breeze rustled in the trees, filtering splashes of sunshine on the water. The brook flowed over rocks and twigs, not allowing anything to deter it or hinder its progress. Deep in her soul, she sensed a whispered, *Peace be still. Peace be still.*

All the frantic clamor of her first waking moments fell away as she closed her eyes and leaned her head against the tree behind her. Her heavenly Father's presence was so real, words were unnecessary.

Nevertheless, she whispered, "I'm sorry about my temper tantrum this morning, Father." She gasped and swallowed hard as the deep pain stabbed at her again. "My choice hasn't changed. Please use my sorrow and suffering to make me like Jesus so I can be a good mother to these children. Help me be a godly role model as Mother has been to the rest of us. Thank you for all the ways you've prepared me for this."

Polly smoothed her hand over her Bible and the faded burgundy diary that had held such treasure for her. "Thank you, Father, for choosing me to be the beneficiary of Sarah's legacy."

The End

AUTHOR'S NOTE

In 1998 my husband, Donn, and I researched the history of our home in Sandy Lake, Pennsylvania, which was over 100 years old. The lives of some of the former residents so inspired me that I decided to write a historical fiction novel based on their lives.

Our former neighbor, 96-year-old Isabelle Dye, said her husband, George, had lived in our house from the age of ten. His mother died in childbirth leaving eight children whom George's oldest sister, Florence (nicknamed Polly), helped her father raise. There was no doubt who the heroine of my story would be.

Later, we learned that Sarah Davis, the woman who had purchased the land where our home was built, had lost five daughters by the time they moved into our house. After Sarah's death and other devastating losses, her last living son, Richard Vance, had been declared a lunatic. Their home was then sold at a Sheriff's sale. What a story that would make.

However, in spite of the fact that the Davis's and the Dye's were real people and that some of the events in this book are true, the characters I've created, conclusions I've drawn and the story I've written are all fiction. Garrett Young and Savannah Stevens, as well as Reverend Caldwell, Mr. Sullivan, Mr. Burns, the Smitley's, Mason Tripley and his daughters, Esther and Delores, did not exist.

However, some residents or professional people who lived in the late 1800's to early 1900's make cameo appearances. These include Dr. T. M. Cooley, Dr. Wilson, Reverend Lawrence, Mr. Boyd, Innis Patton, and the Potter family. The incident with Kitt Potter and the infamous "Dr." Girard or Gerald (depending on which newspaper account one read) actually happened and is recorded in various newspapers on newspapers.com.

It's not known what complications of childbirth took Margaret Dye's life or the life of the child, whose sex is unknown.

Thomas Davis, the husband of Sarah, owned a clothing store in Sandy Lake in the 1800's which his son, Richard Vance (RV), helped him run. The Lake Local newspaper reported that Thomas and Sarah's son, William, had an arm amputated above the elbow on the railroad between Cincinnati and St. Lewis. The rapid succession of deaths prior to R. V. Davis being declared a lunatic are just as Blanche Davis enumerated them in *Sarah's Legacy*. The coffin of the Davis's daughter, Nancy, was purchased from a furniture maker in Warren, PA, leading to the conclusion that she may also have been at the State Hospital in Warren when she died.

Harry and Naomi "Davis" (legally Whitfield) were raised by their grandparents, Thomas and Sarah Davis. Harry and his wife, Blanche, were the parents of Bill and Vance Davis and lived in a little house (long since torn down) beside our garage on Broad Street. Their legal last name, Whitfield, appears on Harry and Blanche's marriage certificate.

Sarah's diary did not exist but helped me weave together the stories of the two families on whom I focused. Documents at the courthouse only contained an X in place of her signature.

Although every effort was made to keep the story historically accurate, some facts were difficult to ascertain. I had a great time researching and writing this book whose setting is Sandy Lake, Pennsylvania, a place I dearly love and lived for many years. I hope you've enjoyed reading it as well.

CPSIA information can be obtained
at www.ICGtesting.com
Printed in the USA
BVHW03s0522200218
508593BV00001B/1/P